Quill's Adventures

in the Great Beyond

John Waddington-Feather

Illustrated by Doreen Edmond

John Muir Publications
Santa Fe, New Mexico

First published 1980 by Hambleside Publishers Ltd, England
Second edition 1988 by Feather Books, England

John Muir Publications, P.O. Box 613, Santa Fe, NM 87504

© 1980, 1988, 1991 by John Waddington-Feather
Cover © 1991 by John Muir Publications
All rights reserved.

Third edition. First printing

Library of Congress Cataloging-in-Publication Data

Waddington-Feather, John, 1933-
    Quill's adventures in the great beyond / John Waddington-Feather.
— 3rd ed.
        p.   cm.
    Summary: Quill Hedgehog and his friends from the Great Beyond
battle the villainous alley cat Mungo Brown and the Wasteland rats
who threaten to destroy the countryside.
    ISBN 1-56261-015-5
    [1. Hedgehogs—Fiction. 2. Conservation of natural resources—
Fiction.] I. Title.
PZ7.W11375Qui   1991   91-20003
[Fic]—dc20   CIP
                                                                 AC

Designer: Marcy Heller
Typeface: Trump Mediaeval and Hadriano Roman
Typesetter: Business Graphics
Printer: Banta Company

Distributed to the book trade by
W. W. Norton & Company, Inc.
New York, New York

To Sarah, Katherine and Anna,
for whom this tale was first told

Upe

A NEW and ACCVRAT MAP of —

Scrobbescine   Ye Olde Ruins of Virocos

Nightshade Cottage (where Witches lived)

Ye Hides where ye Animalfolk observed ye Humanfolk
Ye Caves where Tobias Toad & ye others hid

Islands
Webfoot Island

Magna Mere

Ye Great Mere of Mellowmark

Vnder which was ye Olde Grozzielande   Ye Mystery Marsh
                                            Ye Old Tunnal
Ye Black Wood

Domusland

The Lythe

Ye Wind Sea

Ye Police Station
(of Mick & Mack & Pip Fieldmouse)

Ye Highway where Bert Squirrels Horse bolted

Ye Standing Hills

Over There

Dormouse Dingle   Ye Great Oak

Performed by Doreen Edmond and to be fould by John Muir Publications cum Privilegio Santa Fe.

Ye Hedgehog Meadow (where Quill lives)   Ye Eelbrook

15 of ye Animalfolk Leagues   Heron Islet

Downe

Chapter 1

It was Spring in Domusland, and young Quill Hedgehog knew it. For some time now, he had felt curious little throbbings in his blood that drew him more and more often to the door of his house, at the foot of the Great Oak, to look at the world outside. All Winter when the snow lay thick he had been forced to stay at home, doing little beyond dreaming away the long Winter days in front of the snug hearth of his kitchen. With a pot of tea at his side and boxes of ginger biscuits, he had repulsed all Winter's efforts at invading his warm retreat by planning what he would do when Spring came.

Now he felt the call of Spring in no uncertain manner. Excited impulses dragged him out to the world beyond; a world where buds and flowers gingerly felt the air around before bursting out in a riot of colour and scent. Each beam of sunlight that skipped in at his kitchen window danced about him playfully, till it wheedled him to the dusty panes and invited him to peer at the world outside.

One day he could resist it no longer; he rushed through his living room murmuring, "Time I was off! Time I took to the road again!" Round he went, here and there, rummaging among drawers and chests for this and that, exclaiming "Drat!" or "Bother!" whenever the article he was looking for wasn't to hand. At length he had collected all he wanted. His holdall was full to bursting, and he made for the door, took a final look around his house and stepped outside into Hedgehog Meadow.

A blaze of light caught him in the face as he went through the door. The snow had gone. All was fresh and new. Life hummed, buzzed and whistled noisily, and the thrill of suddenly becoming part of that newness made each spine on his back quiver with ecstasy. He sniffed eagerly at the warm air. Two or three gulps of its freshness were enough to expel the stale Winter from his lungs, and he leapt for joy. He danced such a jig of pleasure right across Hedgehog Meadow that he was well down the lane on the other side before he stopped, breathless, to rest on the bank, calling out greetings to the other animals and birds who were passing by.

"Eh-oh!" he yelled to a couple of blackbirds who were busily threading wisps of grass into a half-made nest. "Isn't it splendid to be out and about again?"

The cock blackbird eyed him sharply for a moment with bright, orange eye, then said something about "Some folks never have a job to do" and "I wish I had time to sit idling about all day doing nothing." Then he flew off making a great pretence of work, gathering more stuff for his nest.

Quill took it all in good part. Nothing could suppress his joy, and he set off once more down the road that stretched in front of him towards a distant range of hills that flanked the Great Beyond, a strange land that Quill had heard about which lay at the borders of Domusland.

Quill had never been over those hills to see the Great Beyond. Indeed, never till this Spring had he ever wanted to visit the place or climb those distant hills, the Staying Hills. Previously, he had seen them only in a blurred and hazy light, as a dim vision around which clouds had always swirled and which mists had hidden. But on that fresh Spring morning they stood out clear and inviting, a challenge to the spirit of adventure inside him.

2

"Go there I will," he said to himself at length, looking at their peaks. "Why should I always pass the Summer months tramping the same old lanes and the same old roads I wander through year after year in the same old pattern? Why should I go on meeting the same old folk and see the same old sights? It's time I broke new ground!"

A mood of rebellion swept through him, and he shouted defiantly to the world at large but to no one in particular. "I'm going to see what lies in the Great Beyond! I am going over the Staying Hills!"

Suddenly a hoarse, raucous voice above him croaked warningly, "I shouldn't if I were you."

Startled, Quill looked up. Seated on the topmost branch of a dead tree was Kraken, the raven, the oldest bird living in Oak Wood, which adjoined Hedgehog Meadow. "Hello, Kraken," he called cheerily when he had regained his composure. "What did you say?"

"I said I shouldn't venture into the Great Beyond if I were you," the old bird replied, turning his grey head sideways to see Quill the better.

"And why not?" asked Quill sulkily, his good humour soured for the first time that day. "Why shouldn't I see what lies over the Staying Hills, when it is the first time in my whole life I've ever had the slightest inclination to seek a change? I always spend the Summer grubbing about our district before holing up again under my tree for the Winter."

Kraken did not answer at once but ruffled his untidy mass of feathers before settling down more comfortably on his branch. He drank in the warm sunshine so casually that Quill thought he had dozed off to sleep, as he so often did these days. But as Quill heaved his holdall over his shoulders and prepared to move off, the raven halted him again with a croak. "Because," he answered, "you have always lived here and life in the Great Beyond is very different, sometimes dangerous."

3

"And . . . and that's exactly why I want to go there," said Quill, though he did not like at all the latter part of Kraken's statement. He wasn't one for danger really. "I . . . I don't want to be an old stick-in-the-mud all my life like some folks I know round here. Just because I've lived here all my life, it doesn't stop me from exploring fresh ground now. I want to travel! I want excitement!"

"You'd be better staying here," said the raven patiently. "It doesn't do to go to places you don't know—and where you may not be wanted."

"But you don't know if you're not wanted unless you go and find out, do you?" said Quill, feeling quite pleased with his slick reply.

"There is, of course, the possibility you may not come back. When folk don't want other folk, they usually take steps to get rid of them. Better stay where you are; far better," said the raven who, before Quill could think up another clever answer, shook the sun out of his feathers and flew lazily away, leaving the hedgehog staring helplessly after him.

"Fiddlesticks!" said Quill, setting off down the road again. "Kraken is jealous because he's too old to travel. That's all he is, jealous because he's stuck here for life and doesn't like to see younger folk getting on. He wants everything to stay just as it's always been."

Muttering these and other expressions of annoyance, Quill walked on, all the more determined to find out for himself what lay over the Staying Hills. But scarcely had the raven flown off, leaving poor Quill a little unsure of himself and wishing the bird's advice had flown off with him, than Quill saw the figure of an old woman hobbling slowly down the lane before him. She leaned heavily on a stick and carried a basketful of herbs she'd picked from the hedgerows. Quill recognised her at once. It was old Widow Dor, Dink Dormouse's great-great-aunt, who lived down the Dingle with the rest of the Dormouse family.

Kraken's wet blanket of advice still draped itself gloomily round him as Quill caught up with the old lady. He wished her good morning as cheerily as he could, but when she enquired where he was off to, the young hedgehog said aggressively, "I'm off to the Great Beyond." Then he added moodily, "And nobody's going to stop me!"

The Dor woman paused and gave him an old-fashioned look. Though she said not a word, her look spoke volumes, and Quill felt ashamed at his outburst. You see, in the Animalfolk world you never speak rudely to elders, even when elders sometimes make you feel inclined to speak rudely to them. So he said, in a much smaller voice, "Leastways, I hope nobody's stopping me. I do so want to see what lies over the Staying Hills."

The old lady put down her basket and took some time removing her bonnet to mop her brow, for the day was growing warmer. Though he dearly wanted to be on his way, Quill knew he would have to hear her out. At length she said, "No one's stoppin' you, m'lad." Quill felt relieved. He'd been expecting her to say something tart, something like Kraken's words, something to put him off; but she put new heart into him when she continued, "When you're young an' the blood's up, that's the time for findin' out things. Sometimes it'll be a hard time, if you're not a good listener. Sometimes it'll be an easy time, if you use your head. That's the way it goes, an' that's the way it's allus gone, for there'd be no moving forward if young folks' blood didn't rise, eh?"

Quill nodded and smiled. Far from stopping him, she seemed to be encouraging him to go on his travels.

"You want my advice, young Quill?" she asked, giving him such a keen look the hedgehog imagined she read his very thoughts.

"Yes, please, Widow Dor," he answered, picking up his holdall to hint ever so gently he wanted to be off.

5

"Then follow your heart, but use your head. Never let one rule t'other. Let 'em allus work together," she replied, tying up her bonnet strings and picking up her basket, as she also prepared to go.

"I'm mighty obliged, ma'am," said Quill, feeling quite his old self once more. "Now if you'll excuse me, I've a goodish way to make before nightfall . . . but I'll remember what you say. Good-bye."

"Good-bye, young man," she said, turning down the by-road leading to the Dingle. "And never lose heart, 'cos you've a pretty steady head!"

Quill laughed at her compliment and gave her a wave, whistling a merry hedgehog tune which sprung readily to his lips, as lively as the spring in his step. Soon his ill-humour and all thoughts of Kraken had evaporated into the warm air. "What a tale I'll have to tell these stay-at-homes when I return," he thought to himself. What a tale he did have, too! It was just as well that he had no inkling of what it was going to be, otherwise he might have turned round there and then.

As it was, he whistled gaily as he tramped along the road that led to the distant horizon. Gradually, as the day wore on, the hills of the Great Beyond became larger and clearer. They were higher than they seemed at first and looked much more rugged. In fact, in his heart of hearts, though he wouldn't admit it, they seemed just a little frightening, perhaps even hostile.

All afternoon he marched on till, like the day, his first flush of enthusiasm began to wane. The nearer the sun inched its way towards the west, the more weary Quill felt. As the sunlight drained from the heavens, so Quill's energy ebbed away. Dusk found him rather cold, very hungry and a long way from home.

"Time I started searching for somewhere to sleep," he said, looking for a likely spot. He sniffed the air to see if it heralded rain, but instead of the heavy mustiness of rain, there came a delightful smell of cooking, reminding him in no uncertain way of the emptiness which rumbled noisily in his stomach. Old Widow Dor had advised him to follow his heart, but it was his nose he followed unerringly right now.

"Sausages!" the first tingling wave whispered. "Fried sausages!" said the next, following closely on the first one. "And chips!" said yet a third, drawing Quill magnetically along the line at the end of which those exquisite smells were being sent up into the still, evening air.

The more he sniffed, the more his mouth watered. His tummy rumbled louder and louder, the more powerful those savoury smells became. Someone in the copse over the hedge was cooking his evening meal, for Quill could smell the homely wood smoke mingling with the cooking of food. A kettle's whistle added its harmony to the music of camp-cooking; a symphony of sizzles, crackles and soft seductive hisses!

Rounding a clump of trees, he peered through a screen of gorse bushes into a small clearing. There in the middle was the most welcome sight he had seen that day—a camp-fire, liberally capped with pans and a kettle all on the point of producing the most tasty meal that a weary traveller could wish for. Lounging nonchalantly alongside the fire, presiding over the meal in solitary splendour, was a tramp cat. He was tousled, down-at-heel and dusty, but he looked a very friendly, well-fed cat and was not without an aristocratic bearing despite his appearance.

Unable to contain the callings of his nose and stomach any longer, Quill stepped forward. The cat was carefully stirring tea in a pot. Quill cleared his throat. "Er . . . good evening," he began.

Now, if you or I had been alone, busy making a camp-fire meal miles from anywhere on a warm, quiet night, and, what is more, if we had had our backs to a silent intruder who suddenly emerged from the brushwood behind us into our solitary world of daydreams, I know, and you know, exactly what our reactions would have been. To say the least we would have been startled. But the cat? He simply looked calmly over his shoulder, continued stirring the tea, smiled amiably at Quill and said in a soft, cultured voice, "Hello. This is a surprise. Do sit down, old fellow, and have a cuppa."

He extended one languid paw towards Quill, who needed no second invitation to enter the comfortable glow of the fire. The cat went on, "My name's Horatio . . . Horatio Julian Augustus Fitzworthy to be precise—but just Horatio to my friends."

The hedgehog took his paw and shook it, saying enthusiastically, "Pleased to meet you. I'm Quill Hedgehog."

Horatio smiled and casually replaced the teapot lid. Then he turned to the fire and went on making the meal. Quill just could not take his eyes off the great frying pan in which sat twelve huge sausages, nestling snugly in their hot bed of fat. They oozed globules of delight, and the more they sizzled, the more freely Quill's mouth began to water.

Without looking up at Quill, Horatio turned them over slowly with a long toasting fork, so that they sizzled more. Unconsciously, Quill rubbed his agonised stretch of tummy and longed and longed the more.

Horatio sensed his hunger. "Care for a banger?" he asked. "I've plenty more in my tuck-bag."

The cat jerked his head in the direction of his belongings which lay scattered about. A great bag, gaping at the mouth to reveal all manner of good things, was slung on a branch nearby. Other gear showed the tramping life which the cat must have led for some time, for he was quite independent and self-contained. Quill needed no second bidding and thanked Horatio for his kindness, telling him how hungry he was and how he had quite

8

*Quill Hedgehog arrives at the enticing camp-fire
of Horatio Fitzworthy*

forgotten to pack up much food in his haste to get away that morning.

"Don't mention it, old chappie," the cat replied. "Always willing to lend a helping paw to the right types, you know. Don't get many of them about these days, though. Now if you'd make a long arm into the right pocket of my haversack, I daresay you'll find another plate and a knife and fork. By the time you've warmed your plate, these bangers will be ready."

The way in which Horatio turned those sausages again sent Quill off at the double. He was at the haversack and back before the sausages could get in a second sizzle. He stood beside the cat, quite unabashedly licking his lips in glorious anticipation.

Horatio served him six beautiful deep brown sausages. Then he dealt him a mountain of golden chips crisped to perfection. Two doorsteps of crusty bread with lashings of fresh butter were next to move in the hedgehog's direction, followed by a pot of steaming tea in a blue-ringed mug.

"Do begin, Quill," Horatio said as he dealt himself some food. "It soon gets cold out here in the open. Don't wait for me."

A starter's pistol could not have got Quill off to a quicker start. He stabbed hungrily at the nearest sausage, quartered it neatly, gave it a hunk of bread to keep it company, then sent it on its way, rejoicing to the depths of his inner being. Huge draughts of tea were taken as the only break and not a word was spoken till the last mouthful had disappeared; till Quill had carefully wiped his plate clean with the last morsel of bread and popped it into his mouth. Having done this, he put his plate to one side, smiled broadly and sat back—full to the ears!

"Can't beat bangers on a night like this," Horatio said, looking into the red depths of the fire.

Quill agreed. His whole body had a comfortable tightness about it, and life at that moment, under the peaceful sky of a warm Spring night, held all the satisfied delight it was originally created for.

"Going far?" ventured Horatio at length, still keeping his eyes on the fire. He was far too polite to ask where the hedgehog was going.

"I'm heading for the Staying Hills and the Great Beyond," Quill replied. "Thought it might make a change from the usual Summer jaunt round my old patch in the Meadow Shire."

Horatio switched his eyes from the fire. At first he idly watched a cloud of blue smoke reach upwards with curling fingers at the sky. Then he brought his gaze to Quill.

"Funny thing, old chap," he said. "I was heading that way, too. Know much about the place?"

"Nothing at all," said Quill. "Started out on sheer impulse this morning—and against all advice, I might add."

Then Quill told Horatio just how it was he came to be travelling to the Great Beyond. The cat listened to him quietly, nodding his head from time to time and occasionally politely asking Quill how he had fared upon the road and whom he had met. The hedgehog ended by telling him how he came to sniff out the sausages and thanked him for the meal.

"Don't mention it, old man," said Horatio. "Seeing that we're both heading for the Great Beyond, how about the pair of us teaming up for our journey?"

"I'd be delighted," said Quill eagerly, for to tell the truth those feelings of fear which earlier had gnawed into his confidence had not quite disappeared. A companion on his travels would be more than welcome. They made their agreement with a handshake and began to settle down for the night. Horatio spread some dry bracken in front of the fire and put on a few more logs. Then the two animals took out their sleeping gear and laid it on the top of the bracken. They wished each other goodnight and snuggled deeply into their sleeping bags.

Soon they were both sound asleep, dreaming the peaceful dreams that only campers can dream. And as they slept before the glowing fire, a huge, full-faced moon joined the million stars in a cloudless sky to shed her quiet light on the silent glade.

Chapter 2

About five o'clock the next morning, a pale, grey light slid gently across the crest of hills away to the east. There it gradually turned into a delicate salmon pink and then, as its intensity increased, a livid red. Countless birds in the tall trees, under low hedges and in the deep thickets stirred uneasily as the first streaks jogged at their sleep. They ruffled the plumage under which they had nestled during the cold night, stretched stiff legs and wings, then, at a silent signal, burst into full-throated song to greet the dawn.

For an hour or so before, Horatio had been awake. He was a light sleeper at the best of times, and the full moon had pulled him from his deeper slumbers. Huddled over the camp-fire he had stared into its dying embers thinking thoughts of his own about the Great Beyond, to which he was no stranger. Indeed no. He had not admitted this to Quill, for the truth was that Horatio was not the down-and-out cat he appeared to be. He was an aristocratic cat of great distinction—and great breadth of mind and feeling.

Quill stirred as the bright light of the morning woke him, and Horatio poked the embers of the fire.

"Good morning," he cried cheerily as Quill poked his nose from the sleeping bag. "Ready for a morning cuppa, old man?" Quill rubbed his eyes drowsily and scratched the bristles on his forehead. For a moment, he couldn't quite recollect where he was, so deep had been his sleep. He had been back in his dreams at his tiny home under Oak Tree, and the surprise of finding himself by a campfire in the middle of nowhere showed on his face.

"Ah . . . Oh . . . good morning, Horatio," he said, "I'm sorry, I didn't know where I was for the minute. You are an early riser. Been up long?"

"Long enough to make you a cup of tea, old fellow," said the other, taking the boiling kettle off the fire and brewing a pot of fresh tea. He passed a steaming mugful to Quill, who took it and warmed his paws round it as he sipped it thankfully.

By now the wood around them was teeming with life as animals started their morning tasks. A colony of rooks rose noisily into the air over to their right, filling the sky with their bent, black wings. Their raucous cries punctuated the other noises which reached the animals' ears as they took their breakfast. Nearer at hand, the sharp rat-tat-tat of a woodpecker drummed through the wood, while above the field that skirted the wood, a lark rose high into the sky, pouring out its stream of song on all below.

Warmed by the sun and his tea, Quill heaved himself out of his sleeping bag and pottered around after Horatio, helping him pack their belongings before they set off on their travels. He was so glad that Horatio had invited him to go with him that he almost fell over himself trying to help his newfound friend. "Oh, do let me attend to the washing up," he said when Horatio poured the remainder of the hot water into a bowl. "After the splendid meal you cooked me, I can't possibly allow you to do the washing up."

Horatio smiled benignly back. Quill was so earnest about it that he allowed him to get on with the washing and drying while he in turn stowed his gear. That done, he turned to the fire and extinguished it, and then the two animals helped each other on with their packs and made for the high road over the hedge.

The warm air had dried out the dew by the time they set off. The atmosphere was fresh, although the heat of the day was already beginning to set in and make the horizon jump and quiver. The animals reached the edge of the field along which the road ran and climbed the stile. The road felt hard and metallic under their feet after the soft turf of the meadow they had just crossed. In the middle distance along the road, a fine haze of white dust rose and gleamed in the sun's rays. In the far distance, this whiteness turned to grey until it was barely visible where the road finally trickled into a cleft of purple in the Staying Hills.

While Quill adjusted his pack, Horatio fixed his gaze on that distant point of the road. It was beyond there that his home lay, and his eyes gleamed at the prospect of return. He became so preoccupied that he failed to notice Quill was ready to start and continued staring at the hills. Quill was puzzled and followed Horatio's stare, but he could see nothing unusual. Quill coughed politely. "Seen something interesting?" he asked. Horatio blinked as if awoken from a trance.

"Yes, Quill. I was looking at the place where the road disappears into the hills. See it?"

Quill said he did.

"Well, just beyond there is the Great Beyond."

Horatio lowered the stick he had been pointing with, and the two animals began walking towards the Staying Hills. They travelled in silence for a time, because Quill sensed that Horatio was still thinking over something very serious. He knew, as all animals know, that he would tell him what he was pondering in his own good time, so he said nothing. After a while, Horatio said, "I suppose you are wondering what there is I find particularly interesting in the Great Beyond, Quill?"

15

Horatio and Quill begin the journey to the Great Beyond

"You were lost in thought a few moments ago, and I suspected it was something to do with that. Have you been to the Great Beyond before?"

Horatio looked more serious than ever and said, "Yes, Quill, I have. In fact, to be quite frank with you, I was born there and lived there for the greater part of my life."

"Oh!" exclaimed Quill, surprised by the cat's reply. "I was told before I set out that the Great Beyond was a very different place from the little wood and the fields where I live. Kraken, an old raven who lives near me, told me to steer clear of the Great Beyond."

"It was a safe enough place up to a few years ago—before they took over," said Horatio.

"They?" asked Quill. "And who might 'they' be?"

"They," the cat went on, "are the Wastelanders who seized control of the Great Beyond several years ago, imprisoning or driving out the peaceful ones who used to live there, myself among them."

Horatio was so upset at recalling what had happened that he could not speak for a few moments; but eventually he went on. "Perhaps I ought to start at the beginning of this sorry tale and let you know the whole story. You can decide for yourself then whether or not you still wish to accompany me on this journey."

"But I wouldn't dream of leaving you now," said Quill, quite hurt that the thought of deserting his friend should have crossed Horatio's mind.

The cat smiled kindly. "You're a good chap, Quill, and it's nice to know you feel like that. But I must in duty-bound tell you the whole story of how I came to be a tramp cat and why I am now returning to the Great Beyond."

Horatio drew himself up proudly. "Once," he began, "I owned a magnificent castle. The name of it, like the name I bear, has come down through the mists of time. Indeed, as long as there has been a Great Beyond, there has always been a Fitzworthy in it. It is a noble name; one I am proud to bear."

"I thought it sounded rather grand," commented Quill. "Much too fine for a tramp."

"Oh, don't mistake me," said Horatio quickly. "It's not that I hold with fine names when there's nothing behind them but their own empty sound. It's simply that if one cannot be proud of one's name, then what can one be proud of?"

"What indeed?" said Quill. "I wouldn't change my name for anything. The Quills have always been fine, upstanding hedgehogs."

"Of that I'm quite sure," said Horatio warmly. "Quill or Fitzworthy, what's in a name? It's the person behind a name who matters. There's many a rogue hides behind a high-sounding name; many a little man behind a big one. But to my story. I hadn't long succeeded to my castle when I decided to travel abroad. I'm an inveterate wanderer, you know, and I had got into the habit of going abroad—to bring new ideas back into the Great Beyond and all that. It doesn't do to be out of touch too long."

"It doesn't," said Quill. "That's why I decided to move this year."

"Well, I made the mistake of leaving my castle and the family affairs in the hands of a lawyer—a treacherous rogue who had long been envious of my heritage and wanted to add it to his own vast wealth. His sole object in life was to acquire money, to make a profit from all and anything. Life to him is one big business deal, and while I was away, he saw his chance and took it."

"What do they call him?" asked Quill.

"Mungo Brown," replied Horatio. "Oh, fool I was, not to see through the rascal!" No sooner was I out of the country than he entered into league with all the unsavoury elements of the Great Beyond, greedy little twisters like himself, made himself their leader, then brought a pack

18

of good-for-nothing folk into the country from Wasteland. He extorted taxes from countryfolk. Those who wouldn't pay him he slapped in prison. Those who began to oppose him he placed there, too. The dungeons under Fitzworthy Castle are full to bursting with innocent people locked in there as slaves for the Wasteland army."

"Where did the Wastelanders originally come from?" Quill asked, as Horatio lopped off a few imaginary Wasteland heads with the walking stick he carried.

"They come from a country that borders the Great Beyond on the other side. Centuries ago, it was a beautiful place so I've been told, rather like our own country; but the people there became greedy. They found new ways of making things by machines and similar contraptions, and they let it go to their heads. They spoiled their land by trying to take too much from it. They cut down its woods, dug deep mines and left slag heaps all over the place. They fouled their rivers and blackened the very air with smoke from the workshops and factories that they covered their land with. Soon their badly built towns became too much for them and wasted away the people living in them. Eventually, of course, the inevitable happened; they used up all their resources, and their country became bankrupt."

"What happened then?" asked Quill.

"They became shiftless and idle, squabbled among themselves till eventually only their army could keep any sort of order in the place."

"But how did they live? What did they live on if they had ruined their land?" asked Quill, quite intrigued, for this was all new to him.

"They sponged on the good nature of the countries about them. We ourselves used to let them have cheap food, for their own farmers couldn't cope with the large population that had sprung up during the period of affluence."

19

"You would have thought they'd have seen what was happening long before it took place and taken steps to do something about it," said Quill.

"They were—and still are—too greedy. They'd rather live in squalor than make their country beautiful again, as long as their pockets are full. Their land is a shambles now—a wasteland. That's how it got its name. I've never been there, but I'm told the whole place is derelict—acres and acres of slum houses and poisoned land."

"And now they've come to the Great Beyond," said Quill sadly.

"Led here by one of our own folk, Mungo Brown, who now has his own army to terrorise our people. But I'll show him I'm not worthy of my Fitzworthy name if I can't drive the Wastelanders out—and Mungo Brown with them."

A distant rumble of thunder sounded over the Hills they were about to climb. It seemed to announce the struggle that lay ahead. By late afternoon they had reached the lower slopes, where they rested a while and stared at the gap at the point the road disappeared. It was darker now and much cooler. A thick mist swirled on top of the peaks above them; but nothing daunted, they started their climb and just before dusk crossed the border of the Great Beyond.

Chapter 3

Quill had his first glimpse of the Great Beyond as they emerged, clammy and wet, from the clouds blanketing the summit of the Staying Hills. The mist had been particularly thick at the top and had made their going difficult and dangerous. It wasn't until they were well down the other side that the hedgehog saw the magnificent view before him. The distance took away his breath, for he could see right across the Great Beyond to the desolate region on the further side where Wasteland lay.

Most of what he saw was farmland, dotted here and there with cosy farmsteads and punctuated with quaint villages that nestled into the well-tilled acres, so much at one with their surroundings they seemed to have grown from the very soil. Already lights were appearing at cottage windows as folk settled down to their evening meal. Here and there, however, in stark contrast, were the beginnings of the industry the Wastelanders were introducing. Ugly collections of drab, concrete houses, all alike, were stuck at the end of a wide concrete road that slashed across the Great Beyond like an open wound from Wasteland. Other colonies of rats were steadily encroaching on the farmland and were building high-rise tenements along branch routes leading off the arterial road. Not far from them, newly built factories were belching smoke into the evening air.

On a mound, in the middle of the Great Beyond, stood Fitzworthy Castle. It would have looked majestic had it not been put to a use that it had not been accustomed to for many centuries—that of a prison. Its subterranean dungeons were now full to bursting, and from its ramparts cannon poked their menacing mouths. Even more offputting were the rats who policed its walls and lounged about armed to the teeth. Its transformation from Horatio's ancestral home to the vile place it had become was too much for Horatio. He took out his handkerchief and blew his nose hard, muttering something to the effect that he hoped the chilly mist hadn't given him a cold.

Quill tactfully turned the other way. He took out a pocket telescope and looked more closely at the castle. A faint rumbling noise came from that direction, and he could see that the rats were raising the massive drawbridge for the night. Little flashes of light began to appear on the battlements, and Quill could just make out the figures of rat sentries taking up their posts.

Swinging his telescope lower, Quill saw the quarters where the garrison lived. The rat police were sitting down to their meal, and a fat cook ladled soup from a pot to the rats who lined up before him.

As well as the police there were rat soldiers, all dressed in the same black uniforms with the Wasteland emblem of a death's-head on their cap badges. They kicked and jostled other animals, who were clearing the tables and swabbing down the floor where the night sentries had finished eating. These latter animals, prisoners, were manacled. There was no mistaking their abject condition as they withstood the bullying of each rat who passed them.

Quill looked a little closer at one of the animals being bullied. He was an otter. He had both hands manacled and had a large, iron ball fastened to his leg on the end of a short chain. Unlike the other prisoners, he was arguing

22

*Quill and Horatio are horrified to see what the Wastelanders
have done to the Great Beyond*

with his tormentors, but there was little he could do to defend himself against the brutal kicks the rats gave as they passed.

"I say," said Quill handing his telescope to Horatio, "who's that fellow you can see through the window there, the window just below the right-hand turret?"

Quill handed him the telescope. It was some time before he found the window, but when he did, he cried out. "Why, that's Frisk Otter! How the scoundrels are tormenting him! They wouldn't dare to do that if he were free. He'd scatter them like ninepins."

Horatio looked a little longer, then passed back the telescope with a groan. He sat down sadly on the grass beside the hedgehog and looked at the filthy mess the factories were making of the land and the scars the houses of the rats and their road had already inflicted on it. For the first time since he had met him, Quill saw a mood of black despair settle on the cat. Horatio buried his face in his paws. "Oh, dear! Oh, dear! It's no use. We'll never get them out. Just look what they've done to everything!"

Quill put a friendly arm round the cat's shoulders. He was deeply moved and tried to cheer Horatio. "Bear up, Horatio," he said. "At least we are free, and there must be others who can help us. They can't lock up the whole population in the castle. Remember your mighty ancestors. You are the leader that people here have been waiting for. And if your cause is doomed, at least let us go down fighting and not give up before we've started."

At this, the cat raised his head. "You're a good chap, Quill, and no mistake. You buck me up no end. Yes," he went on, "I will remember my ancestors—and live up to the family motto, 'Strive to the end!' To the end our quest shall be. To splendid victory or honourable defeat!"

Quill took up Horatio's heroic posture, placing one leg on a convenient rock and raising an arm in the air. "To splendid victory or honourable defeat!" he echoed, looking down over the Great Beyond.

"What's going on down there?" squeaked a shrill voice behind them suddenly. It startled Quill and Horatio. They ducked down behind the rock they were near and held their breaths. In the excitement of the moment they had not noticed three rats come up behind them in the mist, three rats who were border police. They had been patrolling the Staying Hills, but the thick mist had helped Horatio and Quill to come over unseen. As the cat and hedgehog peered cautiously round the edge of the rock, they could just make out the dim form of the rats, who swung their lanterns this way and that trying to locate the voices they had heard.

They looked a vicious trio in their high jackboots. All of them had pistols stuck in their belts and carried heavy cudgels, which they gripped tightly. Their whiskers quivered fearfully as they sniffed the air, trying to pinpoint the scent of Quill and Horatio, and their shifty eyes looked intently into the dusk for the slightest movement.

Horatio turned his own, by now very baleful, eyes first on one and then on the others. Quill could feel the cat's fur stiffen with rage, and he gripped all the tighter the staff he carried. Quill felt inside his holdall for the little truncheon he had there, his blogging-stick. Both of them prepared to attack.

"You take the right one. I'll take the others," Horatio whispered to him. "And 'it 'im!" he added, quite forgetting his aitches in his excitement.

"On their 'eads?" asked Quill, finding the defect catching.

"Yes, on their 'eads, 'ard!"

By now the rats had become very nervous, and one had drawn his pistol. They stuck close to each other, peering and sniffing into the gloom. The senior rat repeated his question—nervously, "Is anybody there? Answer or we fire."

There was no reply. The rats drew nearer and nearer the rock.

They were very close to it when Horatio lobbed a pebble over their heads to distract them. It fell noisily behind them, and they swung round at once, colliding with each other and clanging their lanterns together. One of the lanterns dropped to the ground and went out. In that instant, cat and hedgehog were upon them. They leapt over the rock and pounced.

" 'it 'im!" shouted Horatio, felling his opponent before the rat realised he'd been hit.

"On 'is 'ead 'ard!" yelled Quill, promptly giving another rat a resounding crack on his topknot.

In a flash, all was done. The fight was over. It was as brief as that, and the two elated animals were left shaking hands over the prostrate figures of the Wasteland rats. Panting with excitement and the glow of success, Quill said, "Now what do we do?"

Horatio was already bending over his rats relieving them of their pistols and other weapons. "When they come round," he said, "I'll ask them a few questions—then we'll let them go, having suitably impressed them with our arrival and given them the idea that there are many more of us coming over the frontier. It will give the other rats something to think about at the castle."

Gradually, the stars spinning before the rats began to fade away. A slight moan, followed by "Oh, my poor head!" were the first signs of life. They looked feeble without their weapons and were distinctly less brave. Quill even began to pity them as Horatio shook them roughly to hasten their return to consciousness. A frightened cry went up from them as they realised they were disarmed.

"Oh, please don't hurt us!" wailed the oldest rat. The younger ones merely opened an eye cautiously, paled visibly at what they saw, and lapsed into pretended insensibility again with a weak groan. They soon snapped out of that, however, when Horatio grabbed them by the scruff of their necks and bellowed, "We'll have none of that shamming here! Don't you waste my time. If you don't answer my questions when I speak to you, I'll . . . I'll split you from ear to ear!" I might add that the cat said the latter threat with a wink to Quill. He was no violent creature, but he knew what sort he was dealing with, and the rats soon jumped to. The sham was dropped at once.

"Oh, pl-pl-please don't, sir! I'm only a p-poor little rat. Th-th-the only son of a w-w-widowed mother, sir!" said one.

Quill was completely taken in by this and offered the rat his handkerchief to mop up the tears that filled the young rat's eye. But Horatio kept up his fierce demeanour and demanded, "Who's in charge of Fitzworthy Castle now?"

"President Mungo himself, sir, at present. He came back from his visit to Wasteland last week after making the new trade treaty there."

"Trade treaty?" asked Horatio.

"Yes, sir," said the young rat enthusiastically. "We have made a new trade treaty with the Great Beyond Republic and are going to build them a new capital city and many, many new factories . . ."

"So," said Horatio, jotting all this down in his notebook, "he means to turn our land into another Wasteland, does he? Well, you can tell him from me he's got another think coming." He looked very sternly at the rats, and after questioning them further about troop locations and other matters that would come in useful if an attack were mounted against the castle, he said, "You can tell your friends back at the castle they can look forward to a hot time from now on. Tell Mr. President Mungo Brown that he's in for a most unpleasant run of trouble. Tell him Fitzworthy has come back to claim his own. And woe

27

betide any rat who falls foul of him, for he will not rest till the castle is his again and every one of you rat folk are out—back in your own filthy land!"

A sullen look began to appear on the oldest rat's face, but it disappeared in double quick time when Horatio's angry speech was delivered not two inches from his own pale face. "You c-c-can rest assured, sir, th-th-that your sentiments w-w-will be expressed to the letter, sir," he said, gulping down his fear and touching his cap. Then he said in a very small voice, "Now, if you p-p-please, sir. May we go?"

"Yes, and make it quick!" said Horatio, pointing down the hillside.

The rats didn't need a second bidding. They were on their way in a jiffy and pattered off down the road towards Fitzworthy Castle for all they were worth.

Horatio waited till they were out of earshot, then he turned to Quill, "That'll put the wind up them a bit," he said, laughing. "But now I think it's time we went to earth a while. They'll be scouring the countryside for us tomorrow as sure as eggs is eggs. It'll keep them busy for a day or two, and meanwhile we'll draw up a plan of campaign with a friend of mine they do not seem to have caught yet, if the information those whippersnappers gave me is correct."

"Oh," said Quill, full of curiosity. "Who's he?"

"An old friend not so far from here," Horatio replied. "He's a Woodlander, and he's the wiliest, most cunning old rascal in the Great Beyond—the perfect ally for our new campaign."

Chapter 4

By the time Quill and Horatio had released the two rats, it was night. On the plain below a mist lay, undulating like the waters of some fairy lake under the moon's rays. Above them a clear sky twinkled and throbbed down its light so that with the aid of the lanterns they had taken from the rats, it wasn't difficult to scramble down the hillside. Horatio knew his way well. Quill followed, excited beyond measure and wondering where the adventure was going to lead them. After an hour's sliding and skidding down the hill, they came to the level, and for a while kept close to a wide brook which eventually became the river they had seen. Quill could hear it chattering down at a brisk pace, and he saw its waters rippling in the moonshine. Then it faded away as they entered a thick wood and the going became tougher.

"Watch your step here, old man," Horatio warned Quill as he stumbled unsteadily down an embankment. "It's pretty treacherous underfoot."

Quill drew closer, for the gloom of the wood began to shut out the moon's rays. The further they penetrated, the eerier it became. Strange snappings and cracklings came out of the darkness. Trees took on weird shapes. It was as if they had entered another world—and a very frightening one.

Once, Quill let out a yell and begged Horatio to shine a lantern in his direction. The cat turned quickly.

"Something's got me by the throat!" squealed the terrified hedgehog. "Something wet and slimy!"

Horatio tugged at a clammy piece of ivy that had wrapped itself round prickles at the back of Quill's neck. When he realised what it was, Quill sighed with relief and gave a weak laugh.

"I'm so sorry," he apologised, "but it frightened me in the dark. I couldn't see it, and it did feel so slimy and drippy—like a snake."

Having freed Quill from the trailing ivy and found his hat, Horatio pushed on again, only stopping at intervals to warn Quill of some obstacle or to check his own way. They seemed to have been trudging for ages through thick undergrowth and clutching thorns when Horatio held up his hand and signalled Quill to halt. He placed the lantern on the ground and began to examine the surface of a great rock which jutted out of a tangle of brambles.

Muttering something about, "I thought they wouldn't have rooted out old Brushy," the cat suddenly applied his shoulder to the rock, and to Quill's amazement, there was a click, and slowly and silently the rock swivelled round. Where it had been, the black, gaping mouth of a tunnel confronted the two animals. Grunting slightly from his efforts Horatio stood up, rubbing the grime from his paws.

"Rather neat, don't you think?" he said, picking up his lantern again. "Nobody would have tumbled on that in a month of Sundays, eh?"

"Not even a year of Sundays!" Quill exclaimed.

"Now then," went on Horatio, "let's drop in on my friend. It'll give him no end of a surprise to see me here once more."

They entered the tunnel entrance which the boulder had concealed. When they were inside, Horatio slid the rock back into place, and as he took his lantern and held it on high, Quill had a good look around.

The tunnel they were in was high and sloped gently down as far as he could see. Obviously, it was well used, for just inside the entrance was a niche cut into the wall where there was an old lantern, a burnt match or two and some tallow candles. The floor was trodden firm by the passage of many feet, and the walls were marked where numerous shoulders had rubbed against them.

"We'd best go carefully," said Horatio. "You never know what sort of booby traps he may have rigged up to stop unwelcome visitors penetrating his hideout. He always was a cunning fellow."

Cautiously, they made their way down the tunnel, until Horatio came to an abrupt halt. So suddenly did he stop that Quill collided with him and bounced off onto his back. "Wh-what's the matter?" he asked, picking himself up and dusting himself down.

"Sorry, old chap," said Horatio, pointing to the ceiling. "But I don't particularly like the look of that."

Slung up above them was a wide net, just visible in the rays of the lantern. Anybody but Horatio would have missed it completely. It was draped so that it hung over the centre of the passage, and weighted along its edges were lumps of iron. Had it fallen, it would have trapped any unsuspecting intruder under its meshes and held him firmly captive. A trip-wire cleverly concealed across the passage was connected to the net. Quill and Horatio stepped over it and continued down the tunnel.

Presently they came to a thick, wooden door heavily studded with iron nails and locked tight. A bell-pull hung to one side, and a brass nameplate underneath it said, "B. Fox, Esq. Pull once for attention. THEN WAIT!"

Horatio gave the bell-rope a jerk, and very distantly, Quill heard the faint tinkling of a bell. Nothing happened for a couple of minutes. Then quietly far above them in the wall to their right, the two animals heard the drawing of bolts. There was a soft noise as a secret panel was pulled back. Quill raised his head to see a blunderbuss being thrust through an aperture and aimed in their direction. He pulled on Horatio's sleeve and pointed to it. Slowly, a vague outline appeared in the darkness behind the gun. The whites of two large eyes fell into line behind the hammer which was cocked back. Then one eye closed, and it was clearly taking aim at the animals below when Horatio took off his hat and exclaimed, "Brush Fox! My dear friend Brushy! It's me, Horatio Fitzworthy and my new friend, Quill Hedgehog!"

The aiming eye opened again quickly and very wide, along with its fellow. The blunderbuss was withdrawn, and the sharp snout and whiskers of Brushy Fox came into sight, surprise and delight mingled in his face.

"Christmas chickens!" he whooped. "Horatio Julian Augustus Fitzworthy himself! I'd given you up for lost years ago! Wait a sec and I'll let you both in."

The fox's face disappeared. There was a sharp snap as the sliding panel shut firmly to, then a clicking of bolts. Noises were heard on the far side of the door. Again bolts were withdrawn, a key was turned and the huge door creaked open on its hinges. Brushy Fox rushed out, flung his arms about Horatio and embraced him like a long-lost brother, slapping him heartily on the back. Then he turned to Quill and wrung his hand till it ached.

"I say I am pleased to see you both," he said warmly. "You've no idea how much things have changed since the Wastelanders took over. It's disgraceful the goings-on there are now, downright disgraceful. But let's not discuss that out here. Come in and I'll lock the door. One doesn't feel safe even in one's own house these days."

The fox cast a suspicious glance over his shoulder down the blackness of the tunnel, then, ushering his friends inside, he slammed the door and bolted it fast again.

Quill found himself in an anteroom from which there appeared to be no way out, until the fox, pressing an unseen button, caused the entire wall beside them to move silently to one side. Facing them was a subterranean courtyard which they stepped into. Immediately, it was lit by lanterns of many colours that added more lustre to the brilliant flower beds and rose trees around the perimeter. Gasping with astonishment, Quill stood in the centre of it all.

"My, what a beautiful garden you have, Brushy!" he exclaimed.

"I'm glad you like it," replied the fox modestly. "It's always been my prize piece. I spend hours here. It's about the only thing that keeps me happy these days; pottering about in it. Don't often get the chance to go out and about as once I did. It just isn't safe up there. It's a different place since the Wastelanders came. Hardly recognise some of my old haunts now that they've built over them. What's more, they've got their spies everywhere trying to nab me and some of the other Woodlanders. Fixed a walloping great price on our heads, they have. You never know who's your friend and who isn't now. Can't take too many precautions. That's why I seemed just a little—er—hostile, a moment ago. Sorry and all that, but you'll soon see what I mean when you've been here a while. But, Horatio, let's have a proper look at you, you old devil." The fox held the cat out at paw's length and scanned his features happily. Then he said, "You know, old fellow, you haven't changed a whisker's width. You're exactly the same genial chap you were the last time I saw you. But what on earth brings you back here? It's more than your life's worth if those villains catch you in the Great Beyond."

"I'm well aware of that, Brushy," Horatio answered, "but I simply had to return. What's more," he added fiercely, "I'm not leaving—ever! I'm here to claim my rights, and either the Wastelanders clear out or I perish in the attempt."

33

Brushy Fox in his glorious, lantern-lit garden

"I say, that's very noble of you," said the fox, putting his arms round the cat's and hedgehog's shoulders to lead them across the courtyard into the house. "But it's going to be a hard job, old man, a tremendously hard job. However, you'll not be alone. There are many still free in the Great Beyond who would be only too pleased to have a crack at the Wastelanders, especially we Woodlanders. We're about the last people they haven't fully subdued, though they've given us a harrowing time, I can tell you. But enough of this talk now. Let's get something tasty tucked under our belts, then I'll tell you all that's happened since you went away."

The three animals entered Brushy's kitchen, and having set his guests by the fireplace with something good in their glasses, he busied himself making a meal, for he prided himself on his cooking. It was a splendid kitchen they were in. A Welsh dresser on the far side of the room held a fine collection of plates and pots which winked the brightness of the walls back into the room. Large hams hung from a ceiling among the herbs that were drying there, and great cheeses kept themselves cool in the larder beyond. Brushy was on the move the whole while, nipping to his pantry and back into the kitchen where a pot that bubbled glad tidings (and had done all its life) began to promise them all sorts of good things, as they sat sipping their drinks by the fire.

In that pot was the makings of a stew that whispered wonderful things to them as its smell drifted past their nostrils. To begin with, it suggested strongly that they hadn't eaten for some considerable time, and then it went on to tell them in its own impressive way what goodness was in store for them inside its depths. It suggested, for example, that there, on the boil, were the finest bits of poultry reared on the farms about Brushy's den. It suggested that there, keeping the poultry company, were best French onions and fine English herbs. It suggested that

35

Brushy was a connoisseur at making game stews, and, above all, it simply begged them prepare themselves fully for the treat in store for them. This they did while Brushy prepared their meal. Their mouths watered unceasingly the whole time that pot was on the boil.

"Well," said Brushy at length, taking off his chef's cap and apron, "I think we're ready to start."

He went to the wall opposite and pressed a switch. A white, scrubbed table which fitted flush with the wall began to descend. To Quill's amazement, its legs unfolded and clicked into place automatically. The fox opened another cupboard and took out three neatly folded dining chairs. No space at all was wasted in that underground hideout of B. Fox.

The meal Brushy served to his guests was exquisite. At the end of it, a very full cat and hedgehog had the greatest difficulty in moving from their dining chairs to the armchairs set by the roaring log fire. They sank thankfully into those deep chairs and let the fireglow light up their satisfied faces. For a time no one spoke. They were all too full. They sipped coffee quietly and nibbled after-dinner chocolates.

Presently, when they were given to conversation, Brushy told his guests all that had happened since Horatio was last in the Great Beyond. It was a tale of terrible woe, and it fired them the more with the desire to expel the Wastelanders from their land before it was too late. Soon they were engrossed working on a plan of campaign. Pencils and paper appeared. The heads of the three animals came closer and closer together as they bent over the small table drawing up lists and figures, sketches and maps. It was long after midnight when they retired to bed, but before they did so, they had worked out the first stage of their plan to drive out the rats from the Great Beyond.

Chapter 5

The Hilltop Inn stood at the crest of a steep hill above the river flowing through the Great Beyond. No longer was the river the turbulent stream it had been when it started off in the Staying Hills. Below the Hilltop Inn the river meandered leisurely across the plain and past Fitzworthy Castle, a few miles away. The river was wide and deep, too deep to be forded, and across it spanned an old, single-arched, stone bridge.

Several weeks after Quill and Horatio had arrived in the Great Beyond, a wagon toiled up this hill on its way to Fitzworthy Castle. It was piled high with cannon balls and weapons of all description. In the castle, a great deal of activity had gone on since word of Horatio's arrival had been taken back by the patrol rats. Many rumours had sprung up—as Horatio had intended they should; exaggerated rumours about scores of cats and hundreds of hedgehogs crossing the border to attack the castle. Mungo Brown was frightened, but he wasn't taking any chances and had sent back to Wasteland for this great wagon-load of arms and ammunition.

In addition, he had ordered out the entire Wasteland army to scour the countryside for Quill and Horatio. There was not a corner of the Great Beyond where a party of Wasteland rats were not chivvying and bullying the Great

Beyonders to find out where the cat and the hedgehog were lying low. They even searched through their own drab towns and had the workers there standing in the narrow streets for hours on end while they combed through the miles of alleyways for possible hideouts. But quite safe and undiscovered, they hid out at Brushy's until they had worked out their plan of campaign.

For Quill, however, it became a dull job. He became more left out of the deliberations simply because, of course, he did not know the lie of the land like the others. So one day he decided to put into action a plan of his very own—for he was a most independently minded hedgehog. His plan was concerned with this very wagonload of arms heading for Fitzworthy Castle and which he'd heard, a few days before, was on its way there from a farmer's wife who'd befriended him and whom he'd made friends with this way. While Brushy and Horatio were hard at working out their plans of campaign, Quill went out daily to spy out the land. At first, he didn't go very far, but in time he travelled further and further afield, always keeping well out of sight, for hedgehogs are good at that. He also discovered whom he could trust and whom to be wary of, and the locals in the farms and villages around the Wood soon came to know him well.

Many of them had been bullied by the rats. Some had had their land confiscated, and all who had opposed them had been carted off as slave labour or imprisoned in Fitzworthy Castle. One farmer's wife in particular hated the Wastelanders, for she kept hens to sell eggs at the local market. One night, a patrol of rats guarding a wagon on its way to Wasteland had broken into her larder and stolen all her eggs. Quill met up with her the next morning on one of his jaunts.

"Oh dearie, dearie me!" she wailed, mopping her eyes with the corner of her apron. "We ain't got much to live on as it is. Now them rats has pinched all my eggs an' I

ain't got nothing for market! Why, oh why, don't someone do summat about them dratted rats? I'd give anything
to get even with 'em."

Quill asked which rats had taken her eggs.

"It's them what's gone to Wasteland for a wagonload
of arms an' weapons for the castle. Old Mungo Brown is
scared silly now he's heard Horatio's back an' he's sent
off for more ammunition. He thinks the castle is about
to be attacked an' he ain't taking no chances. If only them
weapons can be destroyed, there's no telling what'll happen. Them rats is as jumpy as monkeys on tacks!"

As he listened to her, the farmer's wife put an idea into
Quill's head. He remembered old Widow Dor's words as
his heart raced madly at the very daring of the scheme
taking shape in his head—but he used his head well . . .
that is, till panic set in. But more of that later.

"When is the wagon due back?" he asked.

"Day after tomorrow," replied the good lady.

"And where would be the best place to waylay this
wagon, attack it," he asked.

The farmer's wife looked across at him quickly, "Why,
you ain't a-thinking of doing it yourself?" she gasped. "It's
too well guarded by all them rats for any attack."

"I wasn't thinking of attacking it," said Quill, smiling
quietly to himself. "Merely helping it on its way."

As she'd been speaking, Quill had glanced up the road
to the top of the hill. Right at the crest he could just see
a building of some sort. He guessed it was an inn, where
the wagon would stop before the final descent down the
other side to the castle. The farmer's wife seemed to read
his mind, for she said, "If I were goin' to have a go at them
rats an' their wagon, it would be up there. You'd be back
in the Wood in no time an' out of sight. But it's no use.
The wagon's too well guarded."

"Have you . . . have you a spare dress and bonnet I could
borrow?" Quill asked timidly, for such a daredevil

scheme had flashed into his mind, he could barely begin to express it.

"Dress! Bonnet!" the other exclaimed; then it dawned on her what he was up to. "You don't mean you're goin' to . . . ?"

"I do," said Quill, and the farmer's wife laughed loudly.

"They'll never suspect you dressed as me! What a clever idea," she said, and with that Quill followed her into the house to try on his disguise.

Two days later, the wagon toiled up the long hill, as the day became hotter. It was guarded by a troop of soldier rats. They marched wearily on either side of the wagon, which creaked and groaned under its tremendous load. A great cart horse strained at the shafts and was urged to increase his efforts by a one-eyed rat-driver who lashed at him with a long whip.

"Get up there!" he piped shrilly at the horse, lashing out angrily. "We've got to get to Fitzworthy Castle before nightfall, and we won't make it by tomorrow night at this rate, you idle brute."

For good measure, one of the soldiers jabbed the horse with his pike and the poor animal broke into a weary trot. All the group perspired freely, and the more they perspired, the more did their evil tempers rise.

Meanwhile, in the yard of the inn, a plump farmer's wife sat herself down on the bench by the inn sign. She carried a large basket of eggs and looked a very contented lady indeed. At least she looked like a lady, with her wide bonnet, well-worn shawl and voluminous skirts. A very close examination, however, would have revealed a sharp bunch of bristles tucked tightly beneath the bonnet from whose depths peered out the sharp features of Quill Hedgehog. Yes, it was Quill, disguised as the farmer's wife and destined to play a part to throw the approaching rat troop into utmost confusion.

All day before, he had reconnoitered the land round about pretty thoroughly, and he had selected the Hilltop Inn as the best place to intercept the wagon. He had told only the farmer's wife of his schemes, for he felt he wanted to contribute something entirely by himself to help drive the Wastelanders out. Brushy and Horatio were excellent friends, but they did tend so to plan things all by themselves and quite unintentionally leave Quill out. Now he was going to show that he, too, could plan tactics—and put them into operation.

He seated himself down and placed his eggs on the table. The frog innkeeper asked him what he wanted.

"Can I get you anything to eat or drink, lady?"

"I'll have a glass of fizzy lemonade," said Quill in his best farmer's wife voice, keeping his face well shielded by the bonnet he wore.

The frog went off and returned with his drink. Quill paid him, and the innkeeper went back inside without so much as a second glance. Quill knew his disguise was perfect then. He sat for a few moments nervously sipping his lemonade and waiting for the wagon to come in sight. He hadn't long to wait. It appeared with a dusty rumble and drew to a halt on the side of the road. Horse and rats were glad of a breather, and the rats drifted over to the inn, leaving the driver holding the horse. Quill stood up as they came into the yard and approached the dusty group. He knew better than anyone how partial to eggs rats are, and when those greedy creatures saw the large basket brimful with fresh eggs, their voices rose to an excited chatter. They jostled around Quill picking up the eggs without so much as a by your leave and were much too intent on stealing them to cast another glance at the hedgehog. Quill made a pretence of protesting.

"Leave my eggs alone. They're all I've got for the market!" he shrilled. But the rats only laughed and told him to be off. It was just what he wanted, and he went over to

The rat leader running off with Quill's eggs

the driver, the one-eyed rat holding the horse and cursing roundly because he couldn't get at the eggs.

"Them soldiers," he snarled. "Them soldiers gets all the benefits and lets us workers do all the work."

"I'll hold your horse while you go," said Quill. "Someone else as well as the military may as well have my eggs."

The rat looked suspiciously at him, and for one horrible moment Quill thought he'd seen through his disguise.

"You needn't worry. I know how to look after horses," Quill went on, giving the cart horse a reassuring pat on the knee.

The sight of the eggs quickly disappearing under the soldiers' paws was too much for the driver. He cocked his one sound eye at Quill and said, "I'll have an egg if it's the last thing I do. Hold onto my horse, lady, and holler if he gets impatient."

Quill took the horse's bridle and the driver went away like a flash. No sooner had he gone than Quill ran round the shafts and released the harness from the horse; then he ran back and led the horse away on the further side of the wagon. Quickly he took the chocks from under the wheels, released the brake and ran to the rear of the wagon. Fortunately, it was just over the crest of the hill, and as he heaved his weight behind it, slowly, very slowly at first, the wagon began to move and then roll down the hill.

The rats were much too intent on guzzling the eggs they had stolen to notice the wagon moving. When they did so, it was too late. A cry of alarm went up from one of them. "The wagon! What's happening to it? It's rolling down the hill! Where's the driver?"

The dismayed driver ran out from the crowd. He stared helplessly along the road as his wagon, gathering speed every moment, plunged madly down the hill towards the bridge. The rats stopped eating and joined the driver in the middle of the road. With bated breath and rooted immobile by the sight of the runaway wagon, they watched

43

it rampage wildly on its mad career. Its wheels turned faster and faster, faster and faster. Every little rut shook its framework violently. Odd cannonballs began to drop off here and there. A shaft caught a hole in the road and was wrenched from the cart with a splintering crunch. But still it rolled on and on, till, crash! Fifteen and a half pairs of eyes blinked as one, as soldiers and driver saw the wagon hurtle straight through the wall of the bridge and plunge into the river beneath. A mass of bubbles seethed to the surface, followed by a few bits of debris—then the wagon was no more!

To a man, the fifteen rats turned on the horrified driver whose one eye rolled with fear.

"We shall be clamped in irons for this!" they shrieked, beating the driver with his own whip and anything they could lay hands on. "Why did you leave the wagon unattended?"

So furious were they with him, that it was a few moments before they became aware of the horse. It stood quietly at the roadside chewing grass, looking quite surprised at all the fuss and bother. The driver was dragged to his feet by the leader of the troop who bellowed, "Who let the horse out of the shafts?"

"I left it with the farmer's wife you took the eggs from," moaned the driver, cowering beneath the cuffs they still rained upon him.

"That woman! Where is she?" demanded the leader. "After her!"

Immediately the Wasteland rats seized their pikes and started sniffing the air, craning their necks and standing high on their legs to listen for any sound which would betray the direction of Quill's flight. A distant crackling from the Wood indicated the way he had gone, and in an instant, the whole pack of rats plunged into the undergrowth in hot pursuit.

Poor Quill, he'd never run so fast in his life. He stumbled wildly down the path ahead of him, hampered by the skirts he was wearing and tripping blindly over roots of trees which seemed to appear from nowhere. Long, straggly brambles caught at his clothes, and the clawing branches of trees clutched at him as he passed by. His bonnet became entangled in the web of twigs overhead, and he struggled violently to release it, tearing madly at the strings about his throat. He left it dangling and pushed onward, hearing those behind gaining on him every second.

In his frantic haste to escape he took the wrong turning and to his horror realised he was lost. His heart thumped madly, and he panicked, trembling in every limb. Nearer and nearer came his pursuers. Their shrill cries filled the air as they found his bonnet and knew they were catching up on him. Quill's legs became heavier and heavier, and his breathing came in gasps. He felt he just had to rest. He couldn't go on. He leaned against the trunk of a tree and faced his pursuers. All was lost, and he was determined to sell himself as dearly as possible. He set his mouth grimly, put his back to the broad oak tree he was leaning on and prepared for the end.

Chapter 6

Then it happened! Just as he expected the first rat to come in sight, the tree behind him gave way. For a split second he glimpsed the sky, the oak leaves and a startled thrush flying off—all between his feet which shot up before him! Then everything went black and he lay in complete darkness. A voice hooted softly but firmly, "Lie still and keep quiet!" Looking up, Quill Hedgehog saw a faint shape standing over him with two large eyes blinking down at him through the gloom. He did as he was told and tried to collect his scattered wits. Vaguely, he could hear the perplexed voices of the rats beyond the wall of darkness which had suddenly appeared.

"Where's she gone?" queried one voice.

"She was here a moment ago. I heard her breathing," another piped up.

"She can't be far away. Spread out and search!" said a third. There was some distant crackling and scrabbling noises as the rats continued their search, but these became fainter until all was quiet.

For at least five minutes, the eyes above him looked at Quill and Quill looked at the eyes. Whoever those eyes belonged to had seen the danger he was in and had rescued him from it, so he knew they were the eyes of a friend. Nevertheless, they were frighteningly large and round.

After a while, a high-pitched voice said, "I-I-er I think they've gone. Hold on a moment and I'll strike a light for you."

The eyes disappeared as their owner turned and fumbled with some matches. A light spluttered in the darkness, then gave way to the steady glow of a lantern. Quill dragged himself to his feet, and as the figure holding the lantern turned to face him, he found himself looking at Hoot Owl.

For a moment the two creatures looked at each other, then very sombrely the owl said, "My word, young man, but that was a near squeak. Those barbarians out there almost had you. But tell me," here the owl looked closely at Quill through his large, tortoise shell spectacles, "tell me, what is the reason for your peculiar garb?"

Quill realised he was still in his farmer's wife disguise and quickly stepped out of the dress he was wearing. He was breathing heavily after his run in those clothes, so the owl offered him a small stool, which he sat on to explain how he came to be fleeing from the rats.

Not a flicker of surprise passed over the owl's face while Quill told his tale. He stood listening solemnly to what the hedgehog had to say, showing no reaction at all until Quill came to the point in his story where the wagon had run into the river. Even the owl had to utter a mild "Tu-woo-o-o" of pleasure when he heard that. He blinked appreciatively listening to the hedgehog tell of the rats' anger and confusion as they watched their cart roll away.

"They'll get into no end of trouble with their master, Mungo Brown, when he hears about it. He's got a terrible temper, especially when he loses money, and those arms will have cost him many pounds."

When he had brought his story up to the moment he was facing the rats with his back against the oak tree, Quill let Hoot take over, for he didn't know what had happened then, though he was beginning to get a rough

Quill tumbles into Owl View

idea. The owl explained how he had been watching from his lookout above.

"I have one or two gadgets up there which can pick up unusual noises in the forest," he said, "and immediately they began to give warning signals, I was on my guard. You see, some of us here have to keep on the alert constantly, otherwise we'd finish up as prisoners in the castle like so many of our dear friends, alas. From my lookout I saw you running down the path outside, and as luck would have it you stood right beneath my tree. Now, ever since those abominable people overran our country, I have had to rig up my home with all manner of devices to protect it. So have many others."

Quill nodded knowingly, remembering the lengths Brushy had gone to protecting his hideout. The owl continued, "One of my little efforts is a neat, false door cunningly fitted into the bottom of the tree. It's operated from my lookout by a system of levers. It was a comparatively simple matter to release the door which admitted you so efficiently—if a little ungracefully. Once you were inside, it sprang back into place, and to all intents and purposes, the tree was a tree again and those brutes who were after you had lost you. But I'm being a very poor host, I'm afraid. Let me welcome you to Owl View, and, if you're quite recovered, we'll go up to my apartments and have a quiet cup of tea before I take you back to Brushy's house."

The owl lifted up a latch, opened another door and asked Quill to follow him. It was obvious that the room Quill had fallen into was some sort of reception chamber, for when he'd passed through the door which Hoot opened, the owl turned a series of keys and drew a vast number of bolts into place to secure the door against any intruders. Moreover, by the light from the owl's lantern, Quill could see a long, spiral staircase ahead of him winding up into the darkness above. They mounted this staircase now.

49

Owl View was a fascinating place. To begin with, the spiral staircase was simply enormous. At intervals along it, odd doors hung back into the gloom and led off to a variety of rooms from some of which came peculiar glugging noises and strange, chemical smells. One room held an engine of some sort, for Quill distinctly heard the hissing of steam and the clank of mechanisms as they passed.

Also at intervals up the gloomy staircase hung oil paintings and faded photographs of learned owls of bygone days. Many of these professorial gentlemen held ancient scientific instruments in their hands, and most of them were in academic dress. They filled Quill with awe as he trundled by them, for never in his life had he seen such a collection of scholars. The wisest person he had ever come across before was Kraken, but he was simply wise and by no means scholarly. Hoot's ancestors, for such they were, had a preoccupied air of otherworldliness about them, an air which hung about Hoot himself. It was clear that Brushy Fox was cunning and his house rigged out in a very clever fashion. But Hoot's thoroughness at security quite surpassed anything Brushy had thought up. Owl View had been made safe by scientific methods passed down through centuries of learning. Moreover, the owl's technology far outshone anything the Wastelanders had, for he put his knowledge to good use, not to profitability.

They reached a huge door near the top of the staircase, and Hoot opened it to allow Quill to enter. Inside was Hoot's vast library. Thick carpets deadened their footsteps as they floated to Hoot's desk on the further side of the room. The desk was littered with all sorts of papers, and to one side of it stood a complicated machine from which stuck out a whole battery of levers and light bulbs. The levers acted as arms, for when Hoot pressed a couple of buttons on the contraption it started lighting up and making the strangest noises. The metal arms began to move, and from the depths of the machine a teapot appeared.

Yet a third arm brought up two teaspoonsful of tea leaves which were emptied into the teapot, and a fourth arm came slowly into view with a kettle already on the boil. Before Quill's eyes the pot of tea was brewed and two cups of tea poured, and treated with the correct amount of milk and sugar, before being handed politely to the astounded hedgehog.

"Thank you," Quill murmured, absolutely fascinated—nay, hypnotised. He didn't take his eyes off the gadget all the time it was working. To his utter astonishment after he had thanked it, a voice crackled from the machine, "Not at all. It's a pleasure." So surprised was Quill he almost dropped his cup, which clattered dangerously in his saucer.

The owl, who had taken up his cup quite casually from the machine while he had gone on studying a document on his desk, looked up and peered over his spectacles apologetically.

"Oh, I'm sorry," he said, "I'd forgotten you were not familiar with my tea-maker. I call him Tea-leaves. He's a little gadget I knocked together some years ago. Saves me the bother of breaking off from my research when I'm in my think tank. Automatically knows when I want tea, you know, but—er—a little off-putting for strangers I must confess." He pressed another switch and a very comfortable chair moved of its own accord from the wall towards the desk. The owl beckoned Quill into it, and the hedgehog sat down—gingerly.

For a time they sipped their tea, Quill with one eye on the tea machine and the other on the arms of his chair, which carried an array of useful gadgets like book rests and sweet boxes, all worked by the flick of a switch or the push of a button. The tea machine now sat motionless by the desk, emitting slight hissing noises from time to time. Hoot, for his part, continued studying the paper before him, quite oblivious to what was going on about

51

him until Tea-leaves croaked at Quill, as he neared the bottom of his cup.

"Would you care for some more tea, sir?"

Quill was startled again but collected himself and said he didn't mind. Immediately, a long, steel arm shot out, took his cup and saucer from him and repeated the performance it had gone through earlier.

"Biscuits?" asked the machine, handing Quill a plate of chocolate biscuits.

"I'm glad Tea-leaves asked you if you wanted anything to eat," said Hoot looking up. "I'm the most terrible host. It's just as well my machines have turned out thoughtful, good-mannered things, not like the horrors the Wastelanders create. Their machines have quite taken over their lives. Did the idiots but realise it, their machines control them now. They organise their whole country around them; that's why they're building these frightful roads everywhere, so that the newfangled mobile-carriers that foul up their own land can be brought over here." The owl sighed sadly and took a sip of his tea. "Not only that, but they've lost all their kindliness, too, the more they've given in to their machines. Everyone friendly seems to have disappeared since the Wastelanders and Mungo Brown took over. We used to have such jolly times in the old days—family gatherings and all that, you know, tea parties and outings, picnics and games. But now . . ." here the owl ruffled his feathers in a melancholy way, "there's nothing. Parties are all spying and prying for the best job-promotion fixes in the Wasteland industries. There's nothing now. You never know who's a friend and who's spying on you. I can count on one foot the number of people I can trust, and we're marked men all of us, all wanted by the Wasteland rats with a price on our heads. It makes life so difficult, and there's really no reason why it should be so."

He drained his cup and waited for the robot to make him another. When it was served, he continued his tale.

"Before the Wasteland people came, we could move freely anywhere and chat with any odd folk we met. But now they issue passes. The Riverbankers are not allowed to mix with the Meadowites, and the Villagefolk are not permitted to meet the Woodlanders. Only spies are given passes to move freely. You can't even pass the time of day without some magpie or crow watching you, then hurtling back to the castle to bring a gang of rats after you. But it will take wiser heads than theirs to catch Hoot Owl."

Quill had seen enough of Owl View to convince him the owl was right. If there was one safe place in the Great Beyond where the rats could not penetrate, that place was Owl View and its countless inventions that kept Hoot secure within and the rats securely out.

The owl pressed another switch on his desk and boxes of after-tea mints appeared. He selected a box of mints and pushed the others towards Quill, who picked out a good sucking mint and sucked away. Between sucks on his own mint, Hoot said, "What we want . . . suck! suck! . . . is a concerted plan of attack . . . suck! suck! . . . on the Wastelanders' stronghold . . . suck! suck! . . . Fitzworthy Castle."

"It's strange you should mention that," said Quill, "because Brushy Fox and Horatio are working out a plan on the same lines."

The owl sucked silently for a moment, then he said, "And I suppose their plan involves attacking the castle from the outside, eh?"

"Yes, it does," replied Quill.

"Storming the walls or rushing the drawbridge, eh?"

"Exactly," said Quill.

"No good at all," said Hoot brusquely. "They'll never do it. There aren't enough of us, and the castle is too well defended."

Rather smugly, Quill agreed.

"Well, I didn't like to tell them, nor would I dream of intruding on their arrangements in any way, but I thought their scheme did seem a bit optimistic and impracticable. Low cunning would be better, I'm sure, than a direct attack."

"Just so," said Hoot. "Low cunning, backed up with scientific knowledge. My mind has been working along those lines for some time, and at long last I believe I've worked out a plan which would enable only a handful of men to capture Fitzworthy Castle. Once the castle falls, the Wastelanders are lost, for the whole population will rally round us when the stronghold goes—especially now their leader Horatio has come back."

The owl reached for the document he had been studying so closely while Quill had been drinking his tea. He motioned Quill to press the button near his right hand and direct the chair nearer to himself. Quill did so, and the chair transported him round the desk where they could both look at the map of Fitzworthy Castle and the area around it.

"You will doubtless recognise various places on this map," said the owl, tracing the landmarks with a pencil. "Here's Owl View—slap in the middle of the wood. There's the Hilltop Inn—and the path you blundered down and took the wrong turning on. And over here, we see the grounds of the castle. Now my plan is this. Instead of attacking the castle from the outside, we shall tackle the rats and Mungo Brown from the inside—where they least expect it."

"But how?" asked Quill.

"Well," said Hoot, "the bigger the surprise, the more successful will be any attack we make. Once we get in there among them, they'll never know what's hit 'em." The owl's eyes flashed momentarily behind his glasses. "We've many old scores to settle with the Wastelanders," he said grimly, "so this plan just has to succeed. Make no mistake, if it fails, it will be the last chance we shall have to drive these wretched fellows from our country. If it fails, the whole civilised way of living that we know is doomed."

"But how do you propose getting inside the castle without their knowing?"

"Ah!" said Hoot triumphantly, "that is a very clever question. One which it will give me great delight to answer." At this point, he ran his pencil along a dotted line which had been drawn from Owl View to Fitzworthy Castle. The line started at the base of Hoot's oak tree, linked up with another line and finished at the site of an old well which lay in the very heart of the castle, the dungeon courtyard. "This line from my house links up with the course of an old drain that used to feed water to the castle's well. Every castle, you know, had a well in olden times. Now what I propose doing is to tunnel to the old pipeline, which is huge, then use that as a shaft so that we can make a secret entry. For the last few weeks I've been working on a new tunnelling machine, and it's almost ready. In fact, if you've finished your cup of tea, we can go down and have a look at it."

Quill drained his cup and followed Hoot out of the library. Before they left the room, the owl pressed another button and the chairs and tea machine slid quietly on their runners back to the sides of the room. Then the animals went to the basement, to the room where Quill had heard the ticking noise when he first entered. Proudly, Hoot opened the door with, "This is my machine workshop." There facing them was a huge, brass cylinder with a conical nose-point that ticked away smoothly. It was beautifully done up and gleamed brightly. Hoot pottered about it from one end to the other, patting the machine and peering under and around it, over it and along it, as he checked each part.

"Not a bad little job," he remarked, beaming proudly at his brainchild. "It should get us through to the pipeline when the time comes. These cutters on the nosecone here can tunnel through the ground like a knife through butter. All we need to help the machine is folk like Matilda Mole and Big Bill Badger. They can shore up the tunnel after the machine's gone through. Working together, we can be in Fitzworthy Castle in next to no time and once there . . . well, that's another question. That's just where a plan of campaign is called for from Horatio and Brushy Fox. It's time, by the way, we set off for Brushy's place now. They'll be wondering where you are. But before we go, perhaps you'd care to see over the rest of Owl View. I always check up before I go out. Can't be too careful, you know."

Quill didn't need a second invitation to look over that intriguing house. Hoot, who lacked many visitors, was only too pleased to show him round, and by the time they had completed their tour, Quill was excited. The whole plan to take the castle had been explained to him, and he was raring to go.

Chapter 7

As we have seen, not all the Great Beyonders were as free as Brushy Fox or Hoot Owl. There was, imprisoned in the vast network of underground passages beneath Fitzworthy Castle, a large, unhappy group of animals whom the Wastelanders had seized for one reason or another. Some of these unfortunate creatures had been there years, ever since the rats had invaded the Great Beyond under Mungo Brown. Others had been imprisoned more recently.

In the latter category was Frisk Otter, who had played a leading role in opposing the Wastelanders after they had overrun the country. For years he had been a thorn in their side and had stopped them gaining control of the River-bank. But they had finally caught him, and, like all the other Riverbankers who had opposed them, he was carried off and locked in the dungeons of the castle.

Frisk was a powerful fellow, quite the strongest of animals living in the Great Beyond, with the possible exception of Big Bill Badger. He had always been regarded as leader of the Riverbankers, and he was a very popular chap. With him in the dungeons were Vicky Vole and Rachel Water-Rat, neighbours who had helped him oppose the invaders. All three of them had been cast into the deepest, dampest dungeons, and to make doubly sure of their imprisonment, a great iron ball had been fastened to their legs. It was Frisk whom Quill had seen through his telescope the first night he had come to the Great Beyond with Horatio.

Being low-bred fellows, the rat troops took special delight in making Frisk perform unpleasant tasks. He was forced to carry huge logs of wood to the kitchens every day and then compelled to clean out the sour, evil-smelling fat from the cookers. And all the while he went about his tasks he was harried and jeered by the rats, especially a certain section of them. Their particular hatred of him started the day he had disgraced them in a fight on the River Road when they had been sent to arrest him. Singlehanded, Frisk had set about a dozen of them and sent them packing, leaving a trail of broken heads and bloody noses behind them. For weeks these rats had been laughed at by the rest of the garrison and had been given low jobs such as cart drivers, baggage carriers and the like which didn't need much courage to carry out.

Frisk had been placed in the deepest dungeon of all, so deep in fact that it was below the level of the moat when the river was in flood. Green slime hung from the walls where the water had seeped in, and the only light that entered his cell was from the bars of the small window in the door looking out into the corridor. At the best of times, it was a dismal place. But when the wind lashed the moat outside, making it echo and re-echo along the gloomy corridors, the dungeons could be positively frightening. The only good feature about his cell was that Frisk could communicate with Vicky Vole and Rachel Water-Rat through the walls of adjoining cells. Vicky and Rachel had been undercover agents, working against the Wastelanders, but someone had betrayed them and they'd been arrested by the secret police.

One night, shortly after he had been put in his cell after the day's drudgery, Frisk was feeling very low. All day he had been washing up the most greasy of dishes in cold water. He was tired and weary, his head rested heavily on his paws and he looked sadly at the large iron ball at his feet. The ankle to which it was fastened ached and was red from the constant chafing. At length, he lifted his head and sighed hugely.

"What wouldn't I give for a fat, juicy trout," he called to Vicky Vole.

There was a soft shuffle on Vicky's side of the wall. "I wouldn't mind just a little sardine," came back the reply.

Both lapsed into silence again as they looked down at the empty plates before them; plates which a few minutes before had contained their evening meal—weak, watery soup and stale bread.

"Just listen to those gluttons upstairs stuffing their fat faces," said Frisk as the din of the Wastelanders at their meal reached the prisoners' ears. Each night the rats fed on the best food in the land, feasting till late into the night on food they had stolen from the farms of the Great Beyond. Each day it fell to the lot of Frisk, Rachel and Vicky to clean up the mess the Wastelanders left behind, for their table manners were shocking and they always left the banqueting hall in a terrible state.

Frisk and Vicky imagined their favourite dishes appearing before them. Frisk saw in his mind's eye a fat, brown trout grilled to a turn, and Vicky Vole saw before her a row of sardines on hot, buttered toast. Then their thoughts were disturbed by the stamping of many feet and the clinking of many mugs above them. The Wastelanders had finished their main course and were beginning their evening festivities, which consisted of singing insulting songs and reciting insulting poems about the Great Beyonders. It was the turn of the feathered Wastelanders to entertain the company that night, and one after another the birds of Wasteland stood up and sang their tuneless songs.

Frisk Otter, Vicky Vole and Rachel Water-Rat in the dungeons

The magpies and the crows were particularly nasty at mimicking and making fun. Odd verses from their songs drifted down into the dungeons. One magpie was in fine form, and his insolent chatter set the whole table laughing. He could be distinctly heard, as he intended he should, by Frisk, Vicky and Rachel. He was greeted by a loud round of applause as he rose to his feet, preening himself before he started. When the applause died down, he bowed to Mungo Brown and said, "Tonight, gentlemen, I have written a little—er—poem about three of our—er—'guests' —the Riverbankers!" Here there was loud jeering. "Rachel Water-Rat, Vicky Vole and our esteemed Otter." Louder, more abusive applause accompanied by whistles.

Frisk, who could hear all this going on, pricked up his ears and gnashed his teeth angrily. The plump trout quite disappeared from his mind's eye in a flurry of angry bubbles. Rachel jumped to her feet and paced furiously backwards and forwards. Vicky waved her fists in the direction of the magpie's voice and piped, "You'd laugh on the other side of your beak if I could get my hands on you, you black-and-white bundle of wind!"

As if he knew—and, indeed, he knew quite well—what the effect of his words would be on the three below, the magpie continued, clearing his throat and fixing his beady eye soulfully on the ceiling. "Riverbank Ode," he began, "by Flash Magpie."

> The three Riverbankers are such fishy folk,
> Rachel Water-Rat, Otter and Vole,
> They're so close to water with dishes to soak
> That they catch all their perch without pole.
>
> Once these Riverbank three were a troublesome lot,
> To us Wastelanders made themselves pests,
> And some Rat boys especially found them quite hot,
> Till we caught 'em and made 'em our guests.

Now in Fitzworthy Castle they lodge safe and sound,
No more with our plans will they tinker,
We keep these three Riverfolk safe underground,
For they swallowed our bait, line and sinker!

An outburst of cheering greeted the end of the magpie's poem, and he sat down amid much back-thumping from his feathered colleagues. They liked to think their contingent was as good, if not better, than most others. More drink was called for, and the party became noisier than ever. The insults against the prisoners became worse, and the rats became more and more arrogant. Just when the clamour was at its noisiest, the doors opened and a bedraggled troop of rats came in, pushing a miserable one-eyed cart driver before them. They looked frightened and downcast. Their very appearance silenced the room. Even Mungo Brown paused in the act of lifting a fat, greasy kipper to his lips and looked in shocked surprise at the rats.

"Well?" he growled, annoyed that his meal had been interrupted. "What do you lot want coming in here like this?"

The chief rat approached and saluted. Then he turned to two other rats and ordered them to bring the quaking driver forward. They did so and hurled him headlong to the ground before Mungo Brown, where he lay snivelling and begging for mercy. Then the chief rat spoke.

"Your excellency," he began, "through the negligence of Driver 187 the load of arms being brought from Wasteland has been lost."

The kipper hanging from Mungo's paws dropped limply to his plate. It took him a moment for the rat's words to sink in, and he was speechless with disbelief. The rat thought it best to speak on.

"Whilst in the execution of our duty, we was resting at the Hilltop Inn on the way here. We was a-taking of refreshments, leaving the care of the arms and wagon with Driver 187. He abandoned his post of duty to join us, and the cart was sabotaged by a hedgehog."

"What!" screeched Mungo Brown, rising angrily to his feet. "All that money we paid out for those arms—lost? Bring your troops and Driver 187 to my room at once and explain how this happened. You're under arrest—all of you! Get out!"

He whirled round from his seat so quickly that his plate of kippers and drink went flying. Then he stormed out of the hall followed by his bodyguard. The troop of rats and driver were now handcuffed by the police rats and escorted from the room to Mungo Brown's quarters. As for the rest of the company, a hubbub of frightened chatter broke out as they wondered what would happen to the rat troop, and they wondered more how the cart and arms had been sabotaged so close to the castle and under such a strong escort. It cast a blanket of fear over the proceedings; so much so that they all lost their appetites and the party gradually broke up as the Wastelanders made their way back to their quarters.

Chapter 8

M ungo Brown's private room had formerly been the smoking room of the Fitzworthys. In happier days very old portraits of the Fitzworthy family had hung about the walls, but, since Mungo had taken over, all these portraits had been pulled down and now lay mouldering away in the cellars. In their place was a series of life-size photographs of the Wasteland leaders, the place of honour, immediately facing anyone who entered the room, being given to that of President Mungo Brown himself. It was an ugly portrait in a huge, ugly frame and was draped with the Republic flag. Mungo positively scowled his own brand of mean fear from it till even the furniture seemed to cower away. All who came into the room had to salute it—and six of Mungo's bodyguards made sure they did.

Mungo Brown was a lean, scraggy cat. He had once been a lawyer; in fact, he had served Horatio's father, old Felinus Fitzworthy, in his younger days, and while old Fitzworthy had been alive all had been well, for he kept a very close, but benevolent, eye on the affairs of his castle and everything else that went on in the Great Beyond, along with other elected leaders of the place. But Horatio was too easygoing, too lackadaisical in money matters, too trusting. He was no match for Mungo Brown when it came to scheming and plotting by underhand means. The result was that Mungo gradually took over more and more control. He was quick to seize every change and formed a secret alliance with the Wastelanders, always a troublesome lot of fellows who had had their greedy eyes on the wealth of the Great Beyond for years. One summer, while Horatio was out of the country, Mungo had seized power, called in the Wastelanders and made himself dictator in the Great Beyond.

Having asserted his control and declared the Great Beyond a republic, he ruled it with a rod of iron and kept the inhabitants well under his heel. He began to exploit it and to build large factories to make more money for himself. The population were forced to work in these factories for next to nothing, and many were driven from their farms and villages to live in the shabby towns he put up for them and the rats, who came in their thousands from Wasteland. Many creatures of the Great Beyond turned traitor and joined him: scoundrels like the magpies and grey squirrels, shifty people at the best of times. Now they became spies and tell-tales betraying their own folk to the Wasteland army and police. It was these traitors who feared Horatio's homecoming most, and the cowardly chatter that went on in their quarters when news of his return reached them had to be heard to be believed.

But they weren't the only ones to shiver in their shoes, oh no! Mungo Brown himself had turned a few shades more yellow under his mangy coat when he first heard the news from the rat patrol which Quill and Horatio had waylaid. He put a huge price on their heads at once and tried to shrug off the unpleasant news, thinking that they would soon be caught. The longer they remained free, the more afraid he became and the more vile became his temper. The last episode which the rat troop told him about turned his fear to terror. For the first time the newcomers had taken direct action against his forces right under their very noses—and got clean away with it! He was furious and stormed up and down behind his desk while Driver 187 and the troop of soldiers marched in.

The miserable bunch crept before him heavily guarded by ugly-looking police rats. Driver 187 had to be carried in he was so afraid, and as they entered, Mungo stopped walking backwards and forth to scream, "You dolts! You idle, good-for-nothing fools. What do you mean by allowing your wagon to be destroyed? What's all this nonsense about disguised farmers' wives and hedgehogs?"

He leaned across the table and leered so evilly into the one, terrified eye of Driver 187 that the poor fellow passed out under the full force of the leer.

"What happened?" Mungo bellowed at the rat who had led the troop. "I want to know!"

The chief rat gulped and started to tell his story again.

"We was stopped in the execution of our duty, Your Excellency, by a hedgehog dressed as a farmer's wife selling eggs . . ."

He got no further. Mungo ran round the table and seized him by the lapels, shaking him till his teeth chattered.

"You . . . you greedy set of gluttons!" he yelled, quite beside himself with anger. "You lost me thousands of pounds for . . . for a few eggs. You'd sell your own mothers for a handful of eggs." He gave the rat another shake or two, then stalked back to his desk. The rat fell to his knees.

"Please, Your Excellency," he wailed, "please, sir, it wasn't our fault. It was his. He left the wagon after I'd ordered him to stay there and guard it."

The rat driver kept his eye firmly closed. He daren't for the life of him open it to look at Mungo, and he listened miserably as the rat leader continued the tale of woe. "We chased the hedgehog into the Wood. I caught a glimpse of him after the bonnet dropped off, and it was him all right—him as come over with the cat you told us about. I thought to myself, I thought, if we catches him, we get ourselves that money you said you'd give, sir, to them what captures him. But try as we might, we couldn't catch him. He just disappeared into the thick undergrowth—or into thin air."

"He just disappeared into the undergrowth, right under your very noses, eh?" scowled Mungo sarcastically. He glared with contempt at the rat, then sat down drumming his fingers on the edge of his desk. No one met his glares, not even his bodyguard, who cuffed the nearest rat prisoner every time he looked in their direction—just to impress. Gradually his scowl gave way to a leer. The leer mellowed into a twisted smile. Finally he sat back smugly in his chair twirling his whiskers and purring softly to himself. There was no doubt at all in everybody's mind he had thought up something particularly unpleasant for somebody.

"I have it," he said at length. "I have it!" As his temper seemed to have calmed, all the rats gave a weak grin to humour him. "You say that the undergrowth, the bushwood was dense?" he asked.

"Yes, sir," the rat leader replied.

"And dry?"

"Yes—very dry."

"Then if we can't find out where they are, we'll make them come to us. We'll smoke them out!" he smirked. "We'll set fire to the Wood! We'll put paid once and for all to any opposition there. Why didn't I think of it before? It'll be so easy. But first you," here he jabbed his forefinger at the rat leader, "you will carry an ultimatum to the Woodlanders. Either they hand over Horatio Fitzworthy and the hedgehog by midnight tomorrow or else I'll bring my army along and burn the Wood down and catch them as they run out—those who manage to get out alive! I'll burn the Wood down anyhow, but they're not to know that now," he concluded maliciously.

"But . . . but they'll capture me!" wailed the rat.

"That's what I want them to do. Then I'll make sure my message has reached them—that Fitzworthy and the hedgehog, though, are to be taken alive."

He took a sheaf of paper from his desk and began writing slowly and deliberately, "To B. Fox, H. Owl and all others living in the Wood. Unless the lawless attacks which have been made on the army of the Great Beyond cease, and unless the impostor H. Fitzworthy and the criminal he has brought with him to the Great Beyond, a certain hedgehog whose name is not yet known, are handed over alive to my troops at Fitzworthy Castle by midnight on the day this message is received, I will send my army, at full strength, to surround and burn down the Wood. Such Woodlanders who escape the flames and are caught will be executed at once as traitors to the Republic of the Great Beyond. Signed: President Mungo Brown."

Having completed his ultimatum, he read it through and sealed it with the official seal. Then he turned to his bodyguards and said silkily, "Send an escort to the edge of the Wood with this rat. Make sure he enters it. The Woodlanders themselves will do the rest once he's in there alone. They'll take good care he doesn't come out again till they've laid their hands on him. It's up to him now to save his own skin, and the only way he can do it is to hand over my message, my greetings to Horatio Fitzworthy. If he can't persuade them to do what it says—he must roast alongside them! Take him out! As for the rest of this idle crew, put them all on bread and water for a month. The rat driver can go in the Punishment Block for a month, too, and he can count himself lucky to get away with so light a sentence."

Imploring him to be more lenient, the rat driver was dragged off to the notorious Punishment Block where all sorts of horrible things were done to the prisoners there. The others of the rat troop breathed with relief that their

Mungo Brown and his bodyguards

own punishment was light compared with the rat driver's, and they filed out silently.

"And now, my friends," he said to his officers and bodyguard, "we'll see what happens. Somehow, though, I don't think Fitzworthy and his hedgehog friend will show up here tomorrow. The Woodlanders are as stubborn as they are foolish. They would rather perish than hand those two over. In which case they will make our task of firing the Wood all the easier, and once it has been burned down, the new city I promised you, Mungo City, will rise from the ashes. Officers, prepare your troops for marching. Tomorrow we burn the Wood!"

The army officers saluted and went off to prepare the morrow's march. Mungo himself remained with his crony, the Chief of Police, chuckling wickedly. He was an evil cat and no mistake, and so pleased was he with the wicked thoughts he brewed in that black head of his, that he downed at least three whole pints of cream with the Chief of Police before he took himself off to bed that night.

Chapter 9

The night that Mungo Brown sent the frightened rat leader to the Wood, the Woodlanders were themselves gathered at Brushy Fox's house for a council of war against the Wasteland invaders. In the fox's huge back kitchen were all the loyal Woodlanders who were determined to drive out the rats. They sat on benches before a table which had been prepared for their leaders.

It was an evening of great anticipation and touching reunion for many folks, who had had to live in hiding all over the country but were now returned for this last offensive. Big Bill Badger was there, as solid and staunch as ever. He was a huge broad-shouldered fellow, a pillar of strength in the Woodland ranks. By him sat Spade Mole, black and stocky, peering at the gathering through shortsighted eyes; smiling amiably at friends he recognised on the front row, nodding vaguely at faces he could not make out further back. There were Frisk Otter's younger brothers and sisters; slim, lithe-limbed animals filled with a burning desire to free their brother and strike at the hated rats who had burned their homes down to build refineries and docks. Behind them were two Meadowites whose homes had gone also. Leap Hare cut a dashing figure, and by him, in grey battle dress was Swoop Hawk, a proud aloof person and terrible in battle. Also present were the fathers of Vicky Vole and Rachel Water-Rat, grimly determined to set their daughters free and punish the Wastelanders who'd arrested them.

The whole room was filled to bursting with a collection of similar animals who had been driven into the Wood by the Wastelanders and whom Brushy had called together to discuss the plans he and Horatio had been working on. They were waiting only for Quill and Hoot and were rather anxious that Quill had been missing for several hours. Indeed, Rhoda Red-Squirrel had been sent out to scour the Wood some time ago. Now they were all very worried about his continued absence.

"Can't understand it," said Horatio. "Took himself off first thing this morning. I thought he was going out only for a stroll, and I told him not to stray too far away."

"Hoot Owl hasn't turned up yet either," commented Brushy, "and it's not like him to be late—especially for a meeting like this."

Just then there was a commotion at the door. Hoot's high-pitched voice could be heard as the sentry there let him in. He came forward apologising for being late and blinking at the bright light of the kitchen. Behind him, much to Horatio's relief, came Quill.

"Thank goodness you've arrived!" exclaimed Horatio. "We were getting worried about you both!"

"No need to, no need to, I assure you," said Hoot, sitting down and polishing his glasses. "The fact is, we have been having quite an exciting day Quill and I, with some Wastelanders. Quill in particular has excelled himself." Quill murmured something inaudible about what he had done being really nothing and bowed his head. He felt somewhat embarrassed, for he did not like the limelight at all.

"What do you mean?" asked Brushy.

Hoot went on to tell how Quill, singlehanded, had destroyed the weapons being taken to the castle. When he finished, a great cheer went up, and the Woodlanders slapped Quill on the back and pressed round to shake his hand. When the cheers had subsided, Quill himself spoke. "Of course, what Hoot has omitted telling you is that I wouldn't be here now but for his timely help."

He explained how Hoot had rescued him just when all seemed lost and he told them about Hoot's plan for entering the castle and taking the Wastelanders by surprise. Hoot, who had his plans and maps in the briefcase he carried, took them out. He showed them the map on which he had drawn the track of his tunnel, and he pinned it up so that all could see it better.

"It wouldn't take more than a few hours," he explained, "for a tunnel to be cut to the old pipeline. Once we reach that, it's a question of only half an hour or so before we're inside the castle."

There was a buzz of admiration for his plan, but before it could grow, the voice of Swoop Hawk cut it short. "It's an excellent plan," he said, "excellent, but . . ." Here he paused to let his 'but' sink in.

"But what?" asked Brushy, a trifle annoyed, for Swoop had a habit of pouring cold water on ideas that seemed most encouraging. What was even more disconcerting was that he was always right!

"But," continued Swoop slowly, "how do we capture the castle once we're inside? Almost the entire Wasteland army is quartered there, and we are but a handful of folk."

Hoot blinked back at Swoop quite unmoved. The rest of the animals looked at Hoot. They were quite unable to offer an answer to the problem Swoop had raised. "A most wise question," Hoot said to Swoop. "I'm glad you raised it. Once we're inside the castle, that is where Brushy and Horatio's tactics come in. I had myself thought of several ideas to get the Wastelanders out, including one rather ingenious plan involving carrying branches of trees, which our small force could hide behind in order to make them think our numbers are greater than they are. That would panic them. It's an idea I picked up reading a play recently which had been written long ago by a famous writer of the Humanfolk."

Hoot turned to Brushy, who in turn looked at Horatio. He for his part turned to those before him and said, "Well, ladies and gentlemen, we're all in this together, and we're open to ideas. Would you all like to consider how to get the Wastelander army out of the castle so that those inside can capture it? For once the castle is in our hands it will be a rallying point for the rest of the Great Beyonders. They will rise to a man and drive out the rats."

Silence greeted his words as each Woodlander there put on his or her largest thinking cap. The silence lasted several minutes; then a small fieldmouse, a most precocious young fellow, thought he had worked out an idea. He had just raised his hand, when the door burst open and a very agitated Rhoda Red-Squirrel entered, quite out of breath. She held a piece of paper in her hand, a piece of paper bearing a great, red seal. It was the ultimatum from Mungo Brown.

"I took this from a rat we caught in the Wood. He wanted to see you personally and was scared stiff. He implored me to speak with you on his behalf and begged me to give you this. Some of the Stoat Folk have got him and are interrogating him outside."

Brushy broke the seal of the message. He read out its contents to the shocked Woodlanders, then he passed it sadly to Horatio. Just when it seemed their ideas for ousting the rats might succeed, they were to be thwarted by this evil plan to burn down the Wood. With dignified pride, Horatio began to speak. "My dear friends, rather than have you make the terrible decision this note demands, I will give myself up to Mungo Brown . . ."

"Never!" bellowed Bill Badger. "We'll die to the last before that happens!"

"Hear, hear!" came the unanimous chorus from the others. "We will fight to the end!" And a great cheer

Rachel Red-Squirrel hands Horatio Mungo's ultimatum

swept through the room which left no doubt of their loyalty.

Wiping something which looked very much like a tear from the corner of his eye, though he afterwards claimed it was a speck which had got in, Horatio continued.

"Nevertheless, though I greatly appreciate your kind thoughts and loyalty, it is the only course left open to me that I can honourably follow. I cannot allow you to suffer on my account. Already the Wasteland army may be on its way to the Wood and . . ."

At this point everyone thought Hoot had gone mad, for he suddenly started shouting, "Eureka! Tu-woo-oo! They've played right into our hands. Can't you see? Once their army is out of the castle, it's wide open for us to take!"

The truth of what he said dawned on them. They cheered again, this time with relief. "My dear chap," said Horatio, wringing Hoot's hand, "you're absolutely right! We've not a moment to spare. We must get to your place at once and start digging."

Following their leaders, the Woodlanders trooped out of Brushy's house to Owl View. They crowded into the basement there and clustered round the glistening machine which ticked deeply on some trestles. Pottering busily round it, Hoot made the final checks of its various parts, murmuring, "Good," or "Tu-woo," when everything reacted satisfactorily. Finally he turned to his friends and said, "Now if some of you stout fellows will help me lower it into place, we'll set it working. Matilda Mole has selected her team of workers to help prop up the tunnel once the machine cuts it out. Now if you'd please give a hand here . . ."

A party of badgers and otters under Hoot's direction pulled the machine on its runners to the trapdoor in the middle of the room. They lifted up the door and beneath it a black pit yawned—the beginning of the tunnel they were soon to dig. Hoot went down first, and the animals above winched the machine down after him. There were some rails on the floor of the tunnel beneath, and piles of other rails were stacked alongside them, ready to be laid as the tunnelling progressed.

"Steady now!" shouted up Hoot from the darkness. "I want the tunneller to be lowered gently onto these rails. The nose-cone must face the wall of earth over there." Lanterns were lit and passed down with Hoot's map. The tunneller sat snugly on the first set of rails, and Hoot lit the burners. The machine hissed and chuffed and puffed itself to life. Its brassy sides gleamed brightly in the light from the lanterns. It seemed as if it was positively bursting to get at the wall beyond and chew the tunnel from it.

Then, with Matilda Mole at his side, Hoot climbed into the seat above the engine and pulled a lever. With a snort of steam, a chuff and a shudder it sprang to life. The nose-cone began revolving, and, as Hoot steered it into the earth wall, it crunched greedily at it, biting massive chunks of soil and rock which were thrown behind, while the Woodlanders worked furiously carting away the debris that the machine threw back. Matilda's team behind it shored up the sides of the tunnel so that the others could follow safely. They would have to work frantically for hours to reach their goal, but victory at least seemed within their reach.

Chapter 10

Very early the next morning, at Fitzworthy Castle, Mungo Brown stood surveying his army and the workers who were on parade in the courtyard below. It was dawn, and they were about to march off to the Wood. He paced up and down on the ramparts waiting for all his men to form up in their respective sections. At the front of his army was a company of hand-picked rats, his stormtroopers, the Black Jackets, and behind them were the other rat soldiers and workers, followed by the magpies and crows. Finally, in charge of the baggage and carts at the rear of the army came the drivers, dull, cowardly folk who kept well clear of any fighting.

It promised to be a fine day, and the sky was cloudless. Early on it had been misty, but the haze had lifted once the sun rose, so that by the time it peeped over the castle walls, it was already growing warm.

Gazing over the countryside round the castle, President Mungo Brown stared at the distant Wood with an evil glint in his eye.

"Finally," he thought, "I am about to crush the last bit of resistance to my rule here, the last piece of land still free. The Great Beyond will be all mine, its riches, its wealth—and its people, cheap, plentiful labour. By tonight, not one house will stand in the Wood, and on its ruins will be built my city, Mungo City!"

His eyes came back to the troops below, and he grinned wickedly at the thought of the destruction they would make. An officer approached and saluted. "Everything is ready, Your Excellency," he said. "We await your orders to march."

Mungo stood on the tips of his jackbooted toes and shouted at the top of his voice, "Forward! To the Wood!"

Orders were barked by the officers commanding each unit, and the drums struck up at the front of the army. Then the army moved off over the great drawbridge and out into the country beyond. Only a skeleton staff of warders were left guarding the place, and, of course, Mungo's bodyguard. He dared not go anywhere without them, he was so afraid—and so hated in the land.

When the last of the troops had left the courtyard, Mungo Brown strolled down to the dungeons to gloat over his prisoners. It was a favourite pastime of his, and it gave him malicious pleasure taunting them with jibes and reminding them that he was the dictator who ruled the Great Beyond now.

"There'll be a few more prisoners down there by tonight," he thought to himself, as the warder let him through the huge, iron door into the dungeon corridor. He made straight for the Riverbankers' cells, for he liked especially to insult them.

"Well, prisoners," he said, "how are your lodgings today? I trust you all spent a comfortable night?"

Vicky Vole and Rachel Water-Rat showed their contempt by turning their backs on him. They ignored him altogether, but Frisk, as hot-tempered as ever, snarled back, "You scoundrel! You yellow, low-bred Alley-Cat! If only I could lay my hands on you, I'd make sure you spent at least one uncomfortable night."

Mungo was angered by Frisk's reference to his being an Alley-Cat. He was very conscious of his low breeding which he always tried to hide by pretending he was descended from aristocratic ancestors. He merely leered at Frisk, though, and continued, "I may as well tell you now that an old friend of yours has arrived back in the Great Beyond, after skulking abroad for some years. Old Felinus Fitzworthy's son has returned. He came back some time ago, but we've kept it quiet."

At this, both Vicky and Rachel spun round. For a moment Frisk was too surprised to speak, then he burst out, "You're lying. You're trying to trick us. Watch him, chaps, he's got something up his sleeve."

Mungo smiled, almost sweetly.

"You flatter me, Otter, " he said. "It isn't everyone who receives such cautious respect. But for once, I assure you, I am being honest. It's strange but it's true. I'm being absolutely honest. You'll find out for yourselves before long."

"What do you mean?" said Frisk, still eyeing him suspiciously. "I'll believe you when I see him . . . here in this castle, though heaven forbid he should be foolhardy enough to try and come here."

"By tomorrow, my friends," went on Mungo, "I hope to grant your wish. At present he's . . . how shall I put it? . . . hiding, with some of the more troublesome Woodlanders. But not for long. Since he has decided to come back to the land of his birth, I, being a hospitable ruler, will be only too pleased to welcome him here and show him round his old home—before he joins his ancestors."

"You mean . . ." began Rachel in horror.

"I mean when he surrenders, and surrender he will if I judge him aright, he will never leave here again once he's caught. He's too dangerous a prisoner to keep alive. I shall have him executed—nobly, as becomes his rank—and buried, with full military honours. We Browns have our code of honour, too, you know."

Frisk and the other two were silent with shock. They were too stunned to speak. Mungo laughed as the otter slumped despondently on the stool. Rachel Water-Rat turned her back again, too lost for words to reply, while Mungo Brown went on and on about his plan to burn down the Wood and build his city there once the Wood had gone.

Vicky Vole was just about to turn away also when a most odd noise caught her attention. At first, she could scarcely believe her ears, for beneath the floor of her cell she distinctly heard the sound of whirring, of a chuffing and a scrabbling. The noise started at the outside wall nearest the moat, travelled steadily in a straight line across the floor towards his door, then disappeared into the courtyard beyond. Her eyes followed the direction the noise was taking, and it was heading straight for the old well in the middle of the yard! Muffled footsteps followed the whirring noise, footsteps so faint that only the sensitive ears of the Vole were able to hear them. These steps also went in the direction of the well, and Vicky looked hard at its broken-down wall. Then she blinked, yes, she actually blinked in disbelief when she saw a head slowly and cautiously raise itself above the wall round the well. A pair of eyes appeared, large, dusty, bespectacled eyes which peered hesitantly round the deserted yard before the rest of the body came into sight. It was Hoot Owl.

Once Hoot had hoisted himself over the ledge of the well, he turned and helped a second figure over the parapet. It was all Vicky Vole could do not to yell out with excitement, for who should appear but Horatio himself. Next came Matilda Mole, then Quill, and the three of them heaved and tugged the bulky frame of Bill Badger out of the well. He was followed by Swoop Hawk, who glared about him in a most fearsome fashion, before helping out the Otter brothers. One by one, the entire Woodland host came out of the well and stealthily made their way to the dungeons, where Mungo Brown, completely unaware of the entry of the Woodlanders, talked on and on and on about what he was going to do to the Great Beyond, what he was going to build and how much money he was going to make from the whole ghastly business.

Then it happened! With a terrible shriek and a war cry that almost roused his long-dead ancestors from their venerable tombs, Horatio raced down the corridor to engage his mortal foe in battle. Mungo turned and gasped. He was terrified and tried to run away. He hadn't managed a dozen paces before Horatio was on him, pummelling and cuffing him to submission, then handing him over to Vicky Vole's cousin to tie him up and lock him away. In a trice, the rat warder, too, was overpowered and all his keys taken. Quill dashed from cell to cell unlocking the doors and releasing the prisoners. Within minutes every imprisoned Great Beyonder was free, had a weapon thrust into his or her hand and had joined the wave of freedom which was rushing down the corridors of Fitzworthy Castle in a great tide sweeping out every Wasteland rat who got in its way.

Oh, what a reckoning there was! What years of bullying were suddenly turned on the rat garrison still left to defend the castle. Not that the rats put up anything like a fight. They were too taken aback, too panic-stricken to organize themselves. Most of all, the sight of Woodlanders like Big Bill Badger, armed with an enormous bloggingstick, bearing down on them, snarling blood-curdling battle cries, were enough to make the stoutest heart quail.

The bodyguards of Mungo Brown were the first to take to their heels. They fled, not bothering to cross the drawbridge, but taking the quickest route out of the castle by jumping over the battlements into the moat, then swimming ashore. Once on land they scattered and were never seen in the Great Beyond again.

But the victory of the castle wasn't the only one that day, oh no. The Wasteland army, ignorant of the fate which had befallen the garrison back at the castle, marched blissfully towards the Wood. It had gone only two or three miles when the very last rat driver glanced over his shoulder and down the long road back. He heard something behind him and saw a cloud of dust, growing in size all the time, coming down the road and bearing down on them. This cloud of dust was joined each moment by tiny figures, men and women, young and old, rushing out of cottages and hamlets through which the rats had just passed. It was the people of the Great Beyond rising in rebellion against the Wastelanders and swelling the ranks of the Woodlanders who had set out in pursuit.

"Eh!" shouted the rat driver in a frightened voice, "there's something coming up behind us that I don't like the look of. Got your telescope, mate?" he asked the rat beside him. He stopped his cart and peered through the telescope. Then he yelled with fear, "Blimey! It's the cat and that hedgehog! They've got a great army at their backs, and they're charging straight at us!"

News of the attack about to take place was quickly passed forward, but before the rat officers could do anything about stopping them, the cowardly drivers all deserted and fled. They knew full well that since the attack came from the rear, they would have to bear the brunt of it! The terror of the rats spread to the magpies and crows, who fluttered away madly, throwing down their weapons and scattering blindly into the surrounding countryside. Even the grim police rats trembled and had to be goaded forward by their officers, themselves a gibbering, nervous bunch by now. So it was that when they saw the furious charge coming nearer and nearer, and when at last they could actually see the faces of the infuriated animals who were heading directly at them, their nerve broke, all sense of order crumbled, and they fled, tumbling madly over each other in their frantic efforts to get out of the way of the revenge-seeking Great Beyonders.

83

The Wastelanders flee!

Like dust before a broom, they were swept down the vile road they had built, chased, harried and smitten whenever they came within reach. Never had they run so fast. Never was an invading force so thoroughly routed. The rat workers were also driven out, taken from the drab houses they had built or were putting up, and sent packing back to their own country, until by nightfall there wasn't a single rat in the whole of the Great Beyond. Within months, even the houses and factories they'd built had disappeared, too.

Weary, but happy with victory, the Woodlanders returned to Fitzworthy Castle with the others. It was almost dark when they returned, but there was sufficient light for them to see the colours of the old Great Beyond flag, once more flying proudly from Fitzworthy flagstaff on the highest rampart. They paused as they saw it and all cheered loudly, greeting Horatio's return to his old home. Triumphantly, he took over his family's castle again and went in, his arm round the friend who had played such an important part in helping him regain it, his friend from Domusland who was cheered all the way—Quill Hedgehog.

Join the
Quill Hedgehog Club

Quill and his friends invite you to join their Quill Hedgehog Club and receive the latest exciting news from Hedgehog Corner.

When you become a member of the club, you will receive a *membership certificate*, a *Hedgehog Club badge*, and *Quill's Club Newsletter*, which is issued four times a year.

You will be among the very first to learn about Quill and his friends' newest adventures and their battles to protect the environment.

To join, just send your name and address and $10.00 to:

> Quill Hedgehog
> Hedgehog Corner
> Fair View, Old Coppice
> Lyth Bank
> Shrewsbury
> Shropshire
> England SY3 0BW

from John Muir Publications

The Quill Hedgehog Adventure Series

*I*n our first series of green fiction for young readers, Quill Hedgehog, an ardent environmentalist, and his animalfolk friends battle such foes as the villainous alley cat Mungo Brown, the Wasteland rats, and the Grozzies.

Quill's Adventures in the Great Beyond
Book One
John Waddington-Feather
5½" × 8½", 96 pages, $5.95 paper

Quill's Adventures in Wasteland
Book Two
John Waddington-Feather
5½" × 8½", 132 pages, $5.95 paper

Quill's Adventures in Grozzieland
Book Three
John Waddington-Feather
5½" × 8½", 132 pages, $5.95 paper

The Extremely Weird Series

*F*ew things of the imagination are as amazing or as weird as the wonders that Mother Nature produces, and that's the idea behind our Extremely Weird series. Each title is filled with full-size, full-color photographs and descriptions of the extremely weird thing depicted.

Extremely Weird Bats
Text by Sarah Lovett
8½" × 11", 48 pages, $9.95 paper

Extremely Weird Frogs
Text by Sarah Lovett
8½" × 11", 48 pages, $9.95 paper

Extremely Weird Spiders
Text by Sarah Lovett
8½" × 11", 48 pages, $9.95 paper

Extremely Weird Primates
Text by Sarah Lovett
8½" × 11", 48 pages, $9.95

Extremely Weird Reptiles
Text by Sarah Lovett
8½" × 11", 48 pages, $9.95

The Kids' Environment Series

*T*he titles in this series, all of which are printed on recycled paper, examine the environmental issues and opportunities that kids will face during their lives. They suggest ways young people can become involved and thoughtful citizens of planet Earth.

Rads, Ergs, and Cheeseburgers
The Kids' Guide to Energy and the Environment
Bill Yanda
Illustrated by Michael Taylor
7" × 9", 108 pages, two-color illustrations, $12.95 paper

The Kids' Environment Book
What's Awry and Why
Anne Pedersen
Illustrated by Sally Blakemore
7" × 9", 192 pages, two-color illustrations, $13.95 paper
For Ages 10 and Up

The Indian Way
Learning to Communicate with Mother Earth
Gary McLain
Paintings by Gary McLain
Illustrations by Michael Taylor
7" × 9", 114 pages, two-color illustrations, $9.95 paper

The Kidding Around Series

*W*ith our Kidding Around series, we are making the world more accessible to young travelers. All the titles listed below are 64 pages and $9.95 except for *Kidding Around the National Parks of the Southwest* and *Kidding Around Spain*, which are 108 pages and $12.95.

"A combination of practical information, vital statistics, and historical asides."
—New York Times

Kidding Around Atlanta
Kidding Around Boston
Kidding Around Chicago
Kidding Around the Hawaiian Islands
Kidding Around London
Kidding Around Los Angeles
Kidding Around the National Parks
  of the Southwest
Kidding Around New York City
Kidding Around Paris
Kidding Around Philadelphia
Kidding Around San Diego
  (Available September 1991)
Kidding Around San Francisco
Kidding Around Santa Fe
Kidding Around Seattle
Kidding Around Spain
  (Available September 1991)
Kidding Around Washington, D.C.

Kids Explore America's Hispanic Heritage

*W*ritten by kids, for kids. Topics covered range from history, festivals, cuisine, and dress to heroes, mythology, music, and language.

Edited by Judy Cozzens
7" × 9", 112 pages, $7.95 paper

ORDERING INFORMATION Your books will be sent to you via UPS (for U.S. destinations). UPS will not deliver to a P.O. Box; please give us a street address. Include $2.75 for the first item ordered and $.50 for each additional item to cover shipping and handling costs. For airmail within the U.S., enclose $4.00. All foreign orders will be shipped surface rate; please enclose $3.00 for the first item and $1.00 for each additional item. Please inquire about foreign airmail rates.

METHOD OF PAYMENT Your order may be paid by check, money order, or credit card. We cannot be responsible for cash sent through the mail. All payments must be made in U.S. dollars drawn on a U.S. bank. Canadian postal money orders in U.S. dollars are acceptable. For VISA, MasterCard, or American Express orders, include your card number, expiration date, and your signature, or call (800) 888-7504. Books ordered on American Express cards can be shipped only to the billing address of the cardholder. Sorry, no C.O.D.'s. Residents of sunny New Mexico, add 5.875% tax to the total.

Address all orders and inquiries to: **John Muir Publications,** P.O. Box 613, Santa Fe, NM 87504, (505) 982-4078, (800) 888-7504.